THE CARROLL FARM FIGHT

THE CARROLL FARM FIGHT

GREG HUNT

FIVE STAR

A part of Gale, Cengage Learning

GALE
CENGAGE Learning®

Farmington Hills, Mich • San Francisco • New York • Waterville, Maine
Meriden, Conn • Mason, Ohio • Chicago

LIBRARY OF CONGRESS CATALOGING-IN-PUBLICATION DATA

Names: Hunt, Greg, 1947– author.
Title: The Carroll Farm fight / Greg Hunt.
Description: First edition. | Waterville : Five Star Publishing, 2017.
Identifiers: LCCN 2016037335 (print) | LCCN 2016049124 (ebook) | ISBN 9781432833077 (hardcover) | ISBN 1432833073 (hardcover) | ISBN 9781432837013 (ebook) | ISBN 143283701X (ebook) | ISBN 9781432833053 (ebook) | ISBN 1432833057 (ebook)
Subjects: | BISAC: FICTION / Action & Adventure. | FICTION / Westerns. | GSAFD: Western stories. | Adventure fiction. | Romantic suspense fiction.
Classification: LCC PS3558.U46768 C37 2017 (print) | LCC PS3558.U46768 (ebook) | DDC 813/.54—dc23
LC record available at https://lccn.loc.gov/2016037335

First Edition. First Printing: February 2017
Find us on Facebook– https://www.facebook.com/FiveStarCengage
Visit our website– http://www.gale.cengage.com/fivestar/
Contact Five Star™ Publishing at FiveStar@cengage.com

Printed in the United States of America
1 2 3 4 5 6 7 21 20 19 18 17

The Carroll Farm Fight

★ ★ ★ ★ ★

PART ONE
THE CARROLL FARM FIGHT

★ ★ ★ ★ ★

CHAPTER ONE

Mel Carroll was in the back stall of the barn helping Belle calve when he first heard the horses come into the yard. Old Rattler would have warned him about the approach of visitors a lot sooner, but Rattler wasn't around anymore. The new arrivals reminded him that he needed to find himself another dog the first chance he got.

Belle was having a hard birth and they'd been at it for hours. Over and over he'd shoved his arm up inside the cow, trying to turn the calf, and now he thought it was almost ready to pull out.

He was covered with blood and slime and shit, but he was used to that and it would wash off. Belle had kicked him once in the head, hard enough to set off bells inside his skull and make his eyes go starry. He had a welt on his jaw that ached like the devil and oozed bright red blood.

Losing the calf would be bad enough, but if Belle died he'd have to get by without milk and butter until he could replace her. That might not be until late fall when he had something to sell or something to trade for another milk cow. But the calf was almost turned.

He didn't take a look when he heard them ride into the yard, or even when they hallooed the house. He couldn't leave Belle.

"Halloo! Anybody about?" a man called out even louder. He didn't recognize the voice.

"Out here in the barn," he answered. He heard three, maybe

four, men approaching, talking among themselves. The barn door hinges squeaked as one of them wrestled it open. From the back stall where he was down on his knees working with Belle he still couldn't see them, nor they him.

"Back here."

"Step out and let us take a look at you," one of the men said.

"Can't do it. I've got about half my right arm up in a cow." Belle shifted to deal with the discomfort and pain, and he moved with her so she wouldn't break his arm.

The men came toward him, and he could tell they were being cautious. One of them thumbed a revolver hammer back. He slowly withdrew his slimy, bloody arm from Belle, and she turned and looked at him with what seemed to be an accusing glance. He rose to his feet on stiff, aching legs and tried to wipe some of the mess off himself with a piece of burlap.

He took a quick, wishful glance at his shotgun, which leaned against a stall door across the middle aisle of the barn. A man with one of those new-style Navy revolvers came into view, pointing it straight as his middle.

"Morning to you," the man said. "What's your name?"

"Mel Carroll."

The man took stock of Mel, then looked down at the miserable cow. The brim of a big felt hat threw a shadow over his eyes, making them unreadable. A thick oily panhandle mustache and heavy beard covered the lower half of his face.

"Looks like you got one stuck there," the man said. By his way of speaking, Mel could tell he wasn't from around these parts.

"Yeah, but I don't think I'm going to lose her," Mel said.

Standing beside the man with the revolver was a younger fellow, not much more than a grown boy really, carrying an old musket and bayonet longer than he was tall. He looked excited and a little scared, as if he expected trouble to start at any minute and wasn't sure how he'd acquit himself.

The third man, standing slightly back from the other two, was older, in his late forties maybe. He wore a uniform, or at least pieces of one, and a sword in a leather scabbard nearly drug the ground at his side. His gray felt hat had a rakish feather in the woven gold band, and his gray wool tunic had fancy gold buttons and gold insignias on the collar.

"The calf was turned and couldn't slide out like it should," Mel explained, in case they were town men and didn't know about such things. "I've been out here since daybreak, trying to help it out. 'Bout got it now."

"Well you don't have to worry about your cow no more," the man with the handgun said. He seemed to smile a crooked smile, although it was hard to be sure under all those whiskers.

"I expect I do," Mel said. There was something about this man that set Mel's nerves on edge, like meeting up face-to-face with a wild animal and not being able to read its intentions. "Who are you men, anyway? A posse?" The one with the revolver could easily be on either side of the law, but probably not the boy or the older man. "You think I've done something?"

"I'm Major Calvin Hess of the Fourth Arkansas Volunteers," the man in the gray coat announced in a high-toned way. "We're doing advanced reconnaissance for our regiment, and we will need your assistance while we're in this area."

"This ain't Arkansas, mister. It's Missouri," Mel advised. "Are you fellows lost? I can point the way back home if that's what you need."

"We know where we are, sir," the major assured him with a huff in his voice. "And we also know that there are two regiments of Missouri regulars and at least one regiment of volunteers moving south to confront us. Since you live here and know this country, we'll need your services over the next few days as guide and scout."

"All those regiments are none of my affair, mister."

The man with the revolver eased up toward Mel, still pointing his handgun at him. "I'll make it simple for you, goober," he said. "There's a big fight shaping up hereabouts, and it's bound to become your affair right quick, whether you want it to or not."

"Maybe so, but I'll have no part of it. Take your fight someplace else."

"Did you hear the major asking, or telling?"

Mel felt the anger rise in him, but tried not to let it show. He figured it wouldn't bother this man a bit to leave him gut-shot and bleeding out right here on the floor of his own barn. And there would be no one to avenge his murder.

"Calm down, Mr. Doolin," the major instructed, quiet but firm. "Our mission here is not to ride roughshod over the civilian population . . . unless provoked."

"Wal Major, he's provoking me already," the bearded man said, wagging the muzzle of his handgun carelessly at Mel.

"Nonetheless, Mr. Doolin," the major said. Then, addressing Mel, he asked, "What was your name again, sir?"

"Melvin Carroll. This is my farm, and you men are no longer welcome here. Regiment or no regiment."

"I'm not interested in whether we're welcome here or not," the major said. "My orders are to enlist the aid of local residents as needed to serve as scouts, which I am now doing with you. And I am also under orders to requisition the horses and livestock in this area for use by the Fourth Arkansas Volunteers . . ."

"The hell you say!" Mel growled.

"We will issue certificates of payment, of course. Our disbursement office in Little Rock will reimburse you at fair market value for the animals taken."

"Little Rock my ass!" Mel said. "No one's taking a single

animal from this farm, not a horse or a cow or even a pullet."
He glanced again at his shotgun, then back at the bearded man.
Both knew what he was thinking, and both knew he didn't have
a whisper of a chance of reaching it. "Now, I've got a heifer
here trying to push a calf out into the world, and she can't do it
without my help. I haven't got the time . . ."

Before he could finish, the bearded man named Doolin
stepped forward, pointed his revolver down at Belle and fired.
Belle's body bucked and she let out one plaintive bleat, a sound
unlike any Mel could ever remember hearing from a cow. Then
she lay still as blood began to ooze from the small hole in back
of her still-open eye.

"Now you got lots of time," Doolin chuckled, "and the boys
will have fresh meat tonight."

After that, everything happened fast.

By the time Doolin began to swing the gun back toward Mel,
the nine-inch blade of Mel's sheath knife was already sliding up
under his breastbone, seeking his heart. Mel accepted the
revolver from the hand of the falling man, almost as a gift.

The youth, to his credit, tried to react appropriately, but the
long musket was clumsy and unfamiliar in his hands. He pulled
the trigger on impulse and his single shot whanged off a rafter
high up in the barn. He tried to swing the weapon around and
bring the bayonet into play, but Mel was too close for that. Gazing at Mel, the kid's eyes were large and teary with fear, and he
drew his breath in shallow huffs.

Mel popped the young man in the forehead with the butt of
the heavy revolver, and he fell backward like a post onto the
hay.

That left only Major Calvin Hess of the Fourth Arkansas
Volunteers, who had lost much of his starch and bluster as he
watched Mel deal with his two underlings. He was backing
toward the barn door, fumbling at the flap of his holster with

hands that had unexpectedly become clumsy, uncooperative things.

"You won't get away with this," Hess said. "You'll be shot for this crime."

"Maybe so," Mel told him. "But your man shot my cow out of pure meanness. He deserved what I gave him."

"You're under arrest for murder," Hess said. "I'll see that you hang for this."

"So is it shooting or hanging, mister?" Mel said. "Which is it that your Fourth Arkansas Volunteers do to men who stand up for themselves and what's theirs?"

Hess seemed to be trying to regain command of himself and the situation, but all hope of that disappeared when he stumbled backward and sat down hard on the ground. The fall popped the holster flap open, and his revolver tumbled onto the hay beside him. Hess reached for it.

Mel didn't own a handgun himself, but he had grown up shooting his father's. Once he had killed a charging razorback with it, which he thought was the best, and probably the most important, shot he had ever made. On impulse he had put that gun in Daddy's right hand before nailing on his coffin lid. It wasn't that he thought a man could take a gun from the grave to heaven with him, or would even need it there. It just seemed like a fitting tribute.

He aimed to shoot Hess in the middle of his head. A body shot was safer but not always as cleanly fatal, and at this distance he thought he could hardly miss the man's head. But Doolin's revolver kicked more than he expected so the round spattered away the right side of the major's skull. Hess ended up dead anyway, but it took him a little longer to cross over.

Mel knelt at the young man's side and checked him for breathing and heartbeat, but found neither. A rattling hiss of air escaped the still body when Mel pressed on his chest, but that was all. Of the three, this was the only one of them that Mel hadn't intended to kill outright, but it wasn't likely that anyone could stay alive with a dent like that in his forehead.

"Well, hell!" Mel muttered, looking at the carnage around him.

Five minutes ago he'd been helping his best heifer push a bawling calf into the world. Now the cow was dead, and the calf might as well be without its mother to succor it.

Plus, he had three dead strangers sprawled out on the floor of his barn.

Mel put his foot on the chest of the one named Doolin and tugged his knife free, wiping it clean on the dead man's shirt before sliding it back into the sheath at his belt. Then he fired a shot into Belle's belly at about the spot where the calf would be. It might be the least of his worries, but it was the easiest to deal with.

Clearly something big was in the wind, and it worried and confused him. All Mel Carroll ever knew much about was the hard simple life he led on these rolling Ozark mountain acres. Even after Mother and Daddy died, he stayed on without any thought of change, rising at daylight, following a mule's hind end down the familiar furrows, eating his simple meals alone, bedding down on the same cot, in the same tight little log home he was born in twenty-two years before.

These mountains in south Missouri weren't such a bad place to live, especially if you'd never known anyplace else. The soil was fertile once somebody put in the hard work to clear the trees, dig out the stumps, and haul the stones away. Daddy had done a lot of that when he and Mother first homesteaded here thirty years ago, and now Mel still added a little to the tillable acreage each year after the spring planting. The wild forested hills surrounding him were downright pretty in the fall. The winter freezes were hard enough to kill the hibernating insects in the ground, but not so harsh that a man spent all winter splitting firewood and feeling miserable.

This war hadn't been much on his mind, and once when a recruiter had come by, he'd hidden in the woods behind the house until the man gave up and left. He didn't feel like heading off to fight himself, not yet, and he wasn't real clear on what the whole thing was about anyway. Besides, the idea of going away, maybe forever, and leaving the farm to lie fallow, unworked and unattended, was a notion he could scarcely bear to consider.

Not much news filtered back this deep into the Ozarks, especially if you weren't looking around for it. Daddy used to buy a newspaper when they went into town, and he and Mother would read it from front to back, sometimes more than once. But now, with them passed on, whatever was in the newspapers was of little interest to him.

There was a town called Palestine several miles down the long winding dirt road that followed the contours of the long valley. It had some stores, churches, a bank, saloons, a livery, white frame houses, and other things that he never had paid much attention to. It was three hours one way down there on the mule, and even longer in the wagon. He seldom made the trip, only when he needed something like an ax or plow, flour and salt, or some similar necessities. He had to take down garden produce or corn, or maybe a couple of kegs of corn whiskey, before he had money to buy anything.

These men meant trouble of one kind or another. There was no doubt about that. But what worried him nearly as much as what to do with them was what the major had said before Mel shot him. There were armies headed this way, one up from Arkansas, and the other down from the north, probably from Independence or maybe even Saint Louis.

Maybe, he hoped, they'd simply pass on by. But he had a bad

feeling in his gut that things might turn out more complicated than that. Until now he had managed to avoid heading off to fight, but now it looked like the fight might be coming to him.

CHAPTER TWO

Mel had carefully considered the location of his new outhouse before digging the twenty-foot pit deep into the ground. It was inside the edge of the woods north and east of the cabin, downwind and far enough away to keep the smell away from his home, but still close enough that those winter morning trips in his panhandles weren't too uncomfortable. The privy was only a few months old, so the pit beneath it was still nearly empty.

He tipped the new wooden one-holer over on its side, then harnessed up Doc, his mule, and drug the bodies up from the barn one at a time. He felt tempted to rifle their pockets for money or anything he could use before dumping them in the hole. But his mother had taught him to respect the dead, and he felt like there might be something in the Bible about stealing from corpses.

So he tumbled their bodies into the hole without searching them first, and threw their hats and guns in after them. Lying in a tangled heap down in the dim recesses of the pit, the bodies of the three men looked small, undignified, and no longer quite human.

Their eulogy was simple. "I'm sorry about this, fellows, but you didn't give me much choice, did you?"

He regretted killing these men, especially the boy, who probably hadn't seen much of life yet, and now would miss out on all the experiences, good and bad, that he might have had. Hess didn't seem all that bad, either, although Mel suspected he was a blunderer and a little too swelled up with the authority he thought he had. As for Doolin, who had started the row and was actually the one responsible for all three deaths, Mel figured that the world might be a little better off without him in it.

But what made them think they could come on a man's land and simply take what they wanted, do what they wanted without any payback? That kind of high-handedness wasn't tolerated in this part of the country, and the local law would never hold him accountable for the ends they had brought on themselves.

But the Fourth Arkansas Volunteers might see it differently if they passed by this way, and he understood that he had to make sure no trace of these men remained on his farm.

He dumped a couple of bags of quicklime that he'd been saving for his garden patch down into the shit hole, then topped it off with a few wheelbarrow loads of barnyard manure and sour hay. They'd probably start stinking in a couple of days even with the lime, but it was a privy. They were supposed to stink. And who else was likely to be around here to smell it?

As he tipped the outhouse back up, it occurred to Mel that it was a sorry sort of tombstone for any man.

The three horses the men arrived on were still tied to the barnyard fence, even though their riders were now on their way to perdition. Two of them were pretty respectable mounts, but the third looked like a broken-down old farm animal. Mel figured that was probably the boy's. There was one nice saddle in the lot, probably Hess's, but Mel knew he couldn't keep any of it, not the horses or the tack.

Riding old Doc, it took Mel most of afternoon to lead the horses deep into the mountainous woods to the west and turn them loose, each a distance apart from the others.

He stopped on the way back and cleaned himself up in Clear Creek Pond. By the time he reached his farm again, the sun was melting into the tops of the pines to the west.

All traces of his three unwelcomed visitors were erased, but he still had a dead cow in the barn, and if he didn't start now, all that meat would be wasted. As he rigged his block and tackle to a beam in the barn and strung Belle up by her hind legs, he planned what he would do to salvage and preserve as much of her meat as possible. He sliced the cow's neck open so any remaining blood could drain out. It would have been better to bleed the carcass out right after it was killed, but he hadn't thought of it, so that was that. Then he fell to work on the skinning and gutting.

Over the next couple of days he'd gorge himself on as much fresh meat as possible, especially the choice parts that couldn't be preserved like the tongue, liver, kidneys and heart. He'd smoke some, and thought he had enough dry hickory in the smokehouse for that. And he'd slice and jerk as much as he could before his salt ran out. He'd have brain cakes for breakfast one morning, a rare treat at slaughtering time, then use the rest of the brain in a concoction Daddy had taught him to make to tan the hide. There were a hundred uses for well-tanned leather around a place like this.

He'd have to work through the night and well into tomorrow to finish all of that before the meat started to spoil. There was work in the fields that really shouldn't wait, but now it had to.

Once Belle was bled out and skinned, Mel used a cleaver, hand ax, and saw to begin cutting her up into more manageable pieces. Those he carried to the long wooden table outside the smokehouse where he would have room to work. When the sun was down, he brought coal-oil lanterns out of the cabin so he could continue working.

By dawn he had made considerable progress on the work, and thought he might be finished by midday. He was stumbling tired now, but if he had energy left when he finished, he still needed to put a few hours into the fields before dark. He could rest all he wanted when the sun set.

Unlike the first three riders who had come upon Mel in the barn unawares, he heard the next bunch approaching a long way off on the other side of the patch of pines that hid the house from the post road. He rinsed his hands at the pump in front of the house, then dried them on a threadbare old shirt that had become a rag. By the time the group of men rode into the yard, he was standing in the doorway of the cabin, his shotgun cradled casually in the crook of his arm. From today on, it would be harder for anyone to ever catch him unarmed.

But there were too many in this bunch to take on, even if he'd had some reason, twenty at least, Mel thought. They stopped in the middle of the yard, ignoring Mel, and surveyed the lay of the farm as if they were preparing to make him an offer for it.

But Mel knew they weren't about to buy anything. They'd take what they wanted, as the first three had tried to do. The head man, mounted on a large, splendid dun, began giving orders.

"Major Sharp, I want pickets in the woods to the north and west. Two squads in each direction, one a hundred yards out, and the other two hundred yards. If contact is made before we've established our positions, their orders are to fight a delaying action as they fall back to the main force."

He wore a gray uniform that looked freshly laundered and pressed, decorated with gold embroidery on the sleeves and collar. Like the man named Hess that Mel had shot in the head yesterday, he had a broad-brimmed gray hat with fancy gold braid and an ostentatious plume. Despite the splendor and formality of his uniform, everything he had on looked a size too big for his wiry old frame.

"Companies C and D will dig in on the west, well past that barn there. A and B will do the same on the north at the crest of the hill, and E will set up their position across that field to the south. Companies F through H will be our reserves here in this open ground where we are, and back along the road. Position sharpshooters in the loft of the barn and as high as they can climb up into those pines. I'll use that shack over there," he added, pointing to Mel's cabin, "as my headquarters, so have my staff start setting up."

Almost as an afterthought, he said, "Major Elliott, deal with that man."

One of the uniformed horsemen separated from the group and rode over to the porch. He was perhaps ten years older than Mel, with a fine handsome beard and a casual, pleasant air about him.

"Morning to you, sir," the rider said. "My name is Major Frank Elliott." Mel nodded, wondering already what "dealing with him" might mean.

"Can I assume this is your farm?"

"It's mine," Mel said.

"And do you live with your family here?"

"Nope, it's only me here."

"Do you intend to use that shotgun you're holding there?" the man asked.

"Sure, I thought I'd do some damned fool thing with it so you can just kill me straight off."

The major grinned and chuckled, lightening the tone between them. "Well until you're ready to start that ruckus, would you mind parking that shotgun against the wall? With our colonel right there in the open, it makes us all nervous to see you holding it."

Mel saw no reason not to do what the man said. He stepped inside the cabin door and leaned the shotgun against the wall, then went back out.

Back down at the bend in the road more men were arriving,

walking four abreast in a continuous line. Mel scowled in their direction, shocked by their numbers and realizing that trouble was definitely in the making here.

"May I ask your name, sir?" the major said.

"It's Melvin Carroll," Mel told him. "What in blazes are you fellows up to here?" Down below the men on the road kept coming and coming, dozens already, maybe hundreds, and no end in sight.

"We're the Fourth Arkansas Volunteers," Elliott told him, "and we'll be needing the use of your farm for a few days."

It was the same unit Hess had mentioned yesterday, but Mel made no mention of it. "And I've got no say in things, I figure," he said.

"I'm afraid not," Elliott said. "But with any luck we'll be moving on soon."

"All right, then. But tell your people not to make too big a mess, and don't go stealing things."

"I can't guarantee that. But let me apologize in advance for any disruption we cause. War, by necessity, is a messy business." Elliott managed to actually sound regretful of the imposition. "We'll need you to keep close by here, but stay out of the way as best you can. If a fight starts, find a place to hide and hunker down until it's over." Mel didn't like the sound of that, not the fight part or the hide part.

"Hopefully at some point we'll be able to let you leave, or move on ourselves. But not right now. We'll want to make sure there's no chance that you'll alert the enemy to our presence."

"I'm not leaving," Mel said. "This is my place."

Some of the horsemen gathered around the leader began to disperse toward the arriving columns of men. Others scattered around the farm, and the rest came forward with the leader as he rode up toward Mel's cabin.

"Major Elliott, have someone take Ranger and the other

horses over to that barn back there and see what feed can be found for them. We'll have some of that fresh meat for supper, and divide the rest among the junior officers. I'm sure there's other livestock around here to meet the needs of the men."

"The hell you say!" Mel stormed, taking a menacing step toward the mounted men. Several sidearms were drawn, and Mel stopped in his tracks. These men were soldiers, and he realized that they wouldn't draw a quick breath before killing him if he gave them reason enough. Killing was what they'd come here to do.

"Colonel Mayfield, this is Melvin Carroll, the landowner," Elliott said. He had shown where he stood by drawing his own handgun at the first sign of threat from Mel.

Mayfield looked down at Mel as if acknowledging some annoying critter. "I regret the imposition, Mr. Carroll," he said. Unlike Elliott, it was clear that he didn't regret a damned thing. "But this is war, sir. My first duty is to my mission and the welfare of my men. They must prepare for what's ahead. We will take what we need and do what we must, and if you don't like it, then you can be damned, sir." Mel considered what a pure pleasure it would be to haul this high-toned old man down from the saddle, grab him by that skinny chicken neck, and give it a quick twist.

Down below they just kept coming. It seemed like the columns would never end. When the open ground around the house, barn, and outbuildings was littered with them, they began to spill into the thirty-acre lower field, oblivious of the long straight rows of corn shoots that had only this week risen a few inches out of the ground. That last rain was what they had needed to make a promising start. But Mel could see that by the time this lot cleared out there wouldn't be a stalk left standing.

"You'll ruin me, mister," Mel announced simply.

"Nonetheless, Mr. Carroll," the colonel told him coldly. There was no need for him to say more.

Mel did a little quick figuring. It would be too late to replant the whole field, but he might make a late planting in the best soil. But where would the seed come from? He'd used up about all he'd saved from last year's crop for the first planting. He still had the bags he'd set aside to grind into meal, but that wasn't nearly enough.

"And where the devil is Hess?" the colonel barked as he stepped down out of the saddle.

The question alarmed Mel because at first he thought it was directed at him. Then he realized the colonel was asking his own staff.

"He should be reporting in soon," one of the others suggested. "He's been out four days now."

"That's too long!" the colonel insisted. "We need intelligence right now about the location of the enemy. I'm blind without him."

"I'll send another reconnaissance party out within the hour, sir," Elliott promised.

"Make it two, Major. One west and one north. I'll hand Hess his own head when he does show up. What's the use of sending scouting parties out if they don't report back when they're needed?"

He's closer than you'd imagine, old man, Mel thought with a sour feeling of satisfaction.

The whole bunch stomped into Mel's cabin as if Mel had handed them the deed to the place. Mel was left alone on the porch, still not quite believing the catastrophe that was unfolding around him.

Down by the road the last of the foot soldiers seemed to have arrived. They were followed by several cannons, pulled by plodding teams of mules, and behind the cannons came a long line of loaded freight wagons.

Far down below, Mel spotted a man coming out of the pasture on the far side of the cornfield, leading Justice, Mel's bull. Justice was so old and fat that he lumbered along behind the man without a sign of resistance, probably hoping there was a bucket of grain in it for him if he came along peacefully.

In his reckless early teens, Mel used to slip down into the pasture, leap astride Justice's back, and hang on for dear life. Justice would buck and leap like the devil had hold of him, but Mel always suspected that the bull enjoyed it as much as he did. Now his age and his ponderous size made it impossible for him to perform his duty with the cows, so Mel let him live out his last years in simple tranquility.

"Poor old fellow," Mel said to himself. He knew what was coming.

When the man leading the bull reached the vicinity of the stopped wagons, he drew a revolver and casually shot Justice in the head. Justice stood where he'd stopped for a moment, let out a confused, mournful wail that Mel could hear even from up at the cabin, and sagged awkwardly to the ground.

But what alarmed Mel even more was the realization that in that same pasture beyond the cornfield were two heifers, five cows, two yearlings, and maybe even two fresh calves that faced the same fate.

There were hoards of men scattered across the place now. Every one of them had to eat, and the meager bounty of Mel's farm seemed theirs for the taking. It was baffling to think that all he owned, everything he had worked for, as well as his parents before him, could be taken, eaten, stolen, or demolished so quickly. And he was powerless to stop it.

Men were busy everywhere he looked, piling up long berms of dirt, cutting down trees for crude barricades, taking over his buildings, arranging their cannons, and laying out their camps.

The meat he had butchered from Belle's carcass and piled up on the table outside the smokehouse had been carried off in a dozen directions. They came and went from the barn at will, taking what they needed, or maybe only wanted.

Every few minutes somebody came out of the cabin and hurried off in one direction or another, and others hurried in to replace them. Messengers, Mel supposed. But he knew that he wouldn't be allowed in there—not allowed in his own home, in the cabin his daddy and mother built thirty years before with two mules, an ax and a crosscut saw, and their own strong backs.

And here he stood like dried cow flop, just letting it all happen. Then an idea came to him. He might not be able to save much of it, but there were some things he could do.

He walked from the cabin down to the barnyard, called Doc to the gate, and let him out. Nobody seemed to notice. The mule had a particular fondness for the acorns that fell from the oaks in the grove west of the barn, and seeing that his owner wasn't calling him into service, Doc headed straight for the trees. With any luck, he wouldn't wander far in the next few hours or days, and wouldn't end up part of a team pulling one of those freight wagons when this lot left out.

Next Mel entered the barn by the back door. The soldiers' horses were in almost every stall, some of them fine blooded animals, munching on his stores of corn, oats and hay. He fit right in with the men coming and going from the barn, and nobody paid him any mind. These men might call themselves soldiers of one kind or another, but few of them had on even any pieces of a uniform. Most wore simple work clothes and boots, much like his own.

He stopped to watch two men with crowbars, his of course, ripping boards off the side of the barn.

"I don't care what they say," one of the men grumbled as they worked. With his unruly shock of brownish blond hair, and

27

skinny wrists and ankles protruding a little too far out of frayed sleeves and cuffs, he reminded Mel of a walking, talking scarecrow. "They oughtn't to split the brigade up like this. One regiment here, another one up north someplace, and two on west. They shoulda kept us together, I say, so we could whup anybody in our way."

"I heard there's ten, maybe twelve thousand of them Missouri boys headed down thisaway," the other man said. He had a wiry tangle of reddish hair and a face deeply pocked from some childhood disease.

"More like twenty thousand, so this lieutenant told me," Scarecrow corrected.

"And here we are, only thirteen hunnert of us, sitting right astraddle of the road they're marching down."

"Yup. If they head thisaway, they'll slice through us like a plow through an anthill."

Looking around at how full his place was with only something over a thousand men there, it was hard for Mel to imagine what the farm might look like after twenty thousand men fought over it.

The barn was nearly stripped of tools, feed, tack, and anything else that might be even remotely useful or worth stealing. But they hadn't completely ransacked the small workroom in one back corner, and Mel found the one tool he needed. The wire cutters were where he always kept them, on the top shelf above the workbench. He dropped them into a trousers pocket and left.

On the crest of the rise north of the house and barn, crews of sweating men were assembling a long barricade of wood, dirt, and anything else they could lay their hands on. Behind that they were digging a long trench four feet wide and three feet deep. To build the barricade, they had cut down a line of tall, straight pines that Mel's daddy had planted close together twenty years ago as a windbreak for the cabin. Mel hated to lose those trees, but at least they would provide him with winter wood close to the house. And he could replant the windbreak.

Beyond the barricade, White Tail Valley stretched away in the distance. It was a beautiful, grass-covered valley bounded on either side by rolling, wooded hillsides. It stretched north from the Carroll farm for a mile or more, then swept west in a long arc, where it continued for many more miles. Before the government cut the road through south of the farm a few years after Mel's parents settled here, White Tail Valley had been a natural route for folks in these parts to travel from one place to another, as it had been for the Indians before them.

It was also a dandy place to plink a deer on a chilly autumn morning, which was why Mel's daddy had named it as he did when he settled here. Years before when they were cutting the Gately Post Road from Palestine to Gately through these parts, Daddy had contended that White Tail Valley was the most logical route. But the road crews had their maps, transoms and compasses, and the map said otherwise. So they had hacked and sawed and dug and leveled their way through the old-growth forest due west from the farm instead. And eventually the new road had crossed Dutchman's Creek on a bridge they built at the far end of White Tail Valley.

But road or not, White Tail Valley would be a logical route to move an army, and these men seemed to be preparing themselves for a possible attack from that direction. Gazing down the long valley, Mel thought that if it was him, he wouldn't attack from out in the open like that, where someone had plenty of time to draw a bead. He'd slink along unseen in the edge of the woods until he was close enough to take the first shot himself. That's the way Daddy had taught him to hunt deer and elk, and he figured it should work as well for hunting men.

But maybe armies fought different, Mel considered. With so

many men a part of it, maybe it wasn't like hunting animals at all.

Staying well clear of the work crews building the barricade, Mel headed east and passed behind his cabin. They didn't seem to expect attack from the eastern side because no fortifications were in the works on that side. He passed through a thin patch of woods into a small clearing where the hog yard was located, well away from the house, and downwind, as mother had dictated.

A hound had little on Mel's mother when it came to a sense of smell, and she had insisted that the hog yard be in the woods well away from the cabin. She liked her ham, bacon, chitterlings and ribs right enough, but otherwise pigs were only stinking, disgusting, grunting beasts to her. None of the soldiers seemed to have been there yet because all his pigs were still accounted for.

Many a time Mel had griped about the long slog down to the hog pen on cold winter mornings. But today he was glad they were where they were. After this he'd see things in a different way. Off from the house and concealed like that, none of the pigs had found their way to the army cook fires, and Mel planned to see that they never did.

He cut the hog yard fence on the east side, away from the house, and buckled a six-foot section back out of the way. Then he went inside the pen and herded them out. It troubled him to turn fourteen pigs, including half a dozen piglets, loose on the land. But what other choice did he have?

If this army had offered to pay him with something more than worthless Arkansas script, he would have sold the whole herd at a bargain price. But he'd rather set them free and let them turn wild than have them stolen from him. At least they'd be out there to hunt someday, and he might even be able to lure some of them back eventually with slops and buckets of fall acorns.

As the pigs began to scatter into the woods, rooting around here and there for acorns, mushrooms and tubers, Mel started walking in a wide circle, first east, then south. He thought it might be dicey crossing the road because of the unaccustomed horse and wagon traffic. But no one challenged him or paid him any mind at all. Everybody's attention seemed to focus west and north, where they expected to face their enemies.

A short while later he was walking outside the split-rail fence that marked the southern border of his land. Far to the north, across the pasture and across the cornfield, he saw that the hill on which his barn and cabin stood continued to boil with preparation for the fight these men seemed to expect. Now that all these intruders had taken over, he hardly recognized the place. But maybe they'd leave soon, and then he could start putting things right again.

It was a fine place to live and work, Mel thought, surveying his farm fondly, as fertile and productive as any in the area. He was born right up there in that cabin, welcomed into the world by his daddy's calloused hands. The farthest he'd ever travelled in his life was twenty-eight miles to the county seat in Winchester, and he'd made that trip only twice. He'd never put money in a bank, and for his whole life he'd never owed another man a single dollar.

But how would all that change, he wondered, if this big fight came about? How much would he have left, or would he even be alive, when it was all over?

Moving from post to post, he kicked loose about thirty feet of split rails, then called the cattle to him with the "Whoo-yah! Heah!" that they knew meant grain, hay, or milking time. As the cattle began drifting toward him, he led them down into the channel of Christmas Tree Creek, named that by his father because of the pretty little cedars that seemed to favor its banks.

A few head were missing. They were probably on their way to the cook pot by now. But maybe some of the remainder might wander far enough away to survive. Rounding up a few head later to rebuild the herd would be better than having none, even if he had to spend a winter or two without beef.

Once his cows were down in the creek cut, out of sight and drifting away, Mel started back across the pasture toward the cabin.

The sun was setting and a low fog was rising, as it often did in the valley this time of year. Usually he welcomed the dusk because it signaled an end to the day's work when he could return to the cabin to eat and rest. Sometimes he'd take a few nips from a clay jug of home brew and twang a few songs on Mother's old guitar.

But today the approaching darkness only made him feel worried and uncertain. He was bone tired, and hungrier than he'd been in a long time. He couldn't recall the last time he had a full meal.

Off to the northwest a distant rumbling rose and faded, then rose again, one thunderclap following close on another for several seconds. That probably meant rain later tonight, or maybe early in the morning. The rain would have arrived at the right time for the corn, if there had been any corn left to rain on. He stopped at the row of trees and brush that marked the division between the cornfield and the pasture to take stock. There was another shallow creek here, a branch of Christmas Tree Creek, and he stooped to raise a handful of water to his mouth.

Low white tents divided up into rows, kind of like streets in a town, covered the eastern half of the cornfield. Men were gathered outside some of the tents, feeding sticks into small fires. They had their muskets stacked together like lodge poles, so Mel figured they must not expect the fight to start any time soon.

During the afternoon they had thrown up a berm of dirt, running from north to south all the way across the cornfield, which was at least three hundred paces wide. They had even blocked the road with a barricade of dirt, apparently to stop the approach of their enemy. On the other side of the berm, all the way to the far tree line, the field was left flat and clear, leaving a broad open killing ground if their enemies decided to attack from that direction.

It was hard for Mel to imagine men who could get themselves so worked up for a fight that they'd run across that much open ground, right at the gunfire of their enemies, simply so they could have at them. But if that other bunch had brought along as many men as he'd heard—twelve or twenty thousand, so those men who were wrecking his barn had said—then he supposed they must have enough for reckless adventures.

Off to the right, down toward the road, some men were cooking in a huge cast-iron pot, even bigger than the one Mel used to blanch the hogs at killing time. The appetizing smell drifting toward him reminded Mel of how empty he was. That would be old Justice he was smelling. Mel drifted in that direction and fell in with a line of men filing past the pot.

When Mel's turn came, he stopped in front of the pot expectantly. The cook serving up the stew was a big, hairy fat man, stripped down to his threadbare undershirt but still sweating heavily. As Mel watched, a rivulet of sweat made its way to the tip of the man's nose and dropped into the pot.

"Yeah?" the man said. He looked Mel up and down like a man examining an imbecile.

"I thought I might try some of that stew you cooked up," Mel said.

"Okay," the man said.

"Okay," Mel said.

They exchanged stares. Mel's look was puzzled, the fat man's annoyed. "So where's your kit?" the man asked at last. " 'Less you want to eat out of your boot. Every man knows you need to have a plate if you're figger on eatin' in my field mess. This ain't Antoine's down in New Or Leens."

"I'm not a soldier, mister," Mel told him. "And the only plates I got are in my cabin up on the hill. But I don't think that sour little cuss with the gold buttons is going to let me in there to get one."

An unexpected smile spread across the man's jowly features and his layers of blubber shook with laughter, slinging sweat in all directions. "So this is your place we're squatting on?"

"My place, and my bull boiled up in that pot. So do you have something around here a man might eat out of besides a boot?"

"I s'pose we can find you something. But I best warn you, that's a mighty tough bull you had there. Eatin' him is like chewing on a belt."

Mel left the line with a tin plate of stew, a hunk of cornbread the size of his hand, and a wooden spoon to eat with. The fat cook had called his concoction "cush," an odd but tasty mix of beef, vegetables, fruit and crumbled cornbread. He settled on the ground near a cluster of men who had finished their supper and were passing around a quart jar half full of pale, tea-colored liquid. Mel knew what must be in the jar by the grimace each man made after he took a swallow.

Off to the west the distant rumblings started again, sounding like an odd succession of thunderclaps. It was full dark now, and Mel was puzzled that he hadn't noticed any lightning flashes in the western sky. He started to say something about the rain blowing in their direction, but was soon glad he hadn't showed his ignorance.

"Sounds like General Willard must be getting thumped over

there by somebody's big guns," one of the men commented. "Either that, or he's doing some thumping hisself."

To a man, they all stared westward, their faces betraying varying emotions.

"Whatever's happening," another in the group said, "seems like it's moving this away, don't it?" He was younger than the others, hardly looking old enough to be a soldier. "Don't it seem closer than a while ago?" He looked from face to face, but nobody offered an opinion.

There was another spate of rumblings, and Mel understood this time that he wasn't hearing thunder.

"Maybe they're cleaning out their barrels for a scrap in the morning," a man in his thirties suggested.

"Or shooting at owls," another chuckled. He must be the funny one in the bunch. "Nothing like twelve pounds of cannister shot to bring a pesky hoot owl down out of the sky."

"More likely there's some men dying over there." The man who made that sober suggestion was older than the rest. If the jittery youth looked too young to be here, this man seemed too old. "Nobody would be fighting like that in the dark unless they wasn't left with no other choice."

They all contemplated that, including Mel.

Common sense told Mel that he should leave the farm right now, tonight, before the fighting moved this way, as this whole army seemed to expect. But he couldn't bring himself to do it. Part of it was simply a young man's curiosity and eagerness to see firsthand what a war looked like. But that old Carroll stubbornness was working on him, too. This was his place, all he had, and if it was getting dug up, ransacked, fought over, blown up and ripped apart, he felt like he needed to be here and know about it. He wished he'd been able to retrieve his shotgun out of his cabin before that little chicken-necked man took it over. At a time like this, a man felt plain old naked without some kind of gun in his hands.

"Anybody know where they dug the shitters?" the older man asked. "I still got the whoopsies from that purple beef they fed us down in Jasper. Going on two weeks now."

"Back by the road, the way we come in," somebody told him. "Downwind for a change."

The old man stood up and said, "I need another snort of that stump water first."

Mel edged forward as the jar started around, and nobody begrudged him a swallow. It wasn't as smooth as the stuff he and Daddy cooked up from time to time, but it would do tonight. His own jug was tucked away in a corner of the cabin, unless those men up there had already found it.

He wandered away, heading up the hill toward the cabin, but he couldn't go near it now. They had pitched several tents in the front yard of the cabin, some of them as big as a room. Uniformed guards with new-looking rifles were posted all around, and the first one Mel approached stepped directly in his path.

"State your business," the guard said. He wore a gray tunic and gray trousers, and held his rifle crossways of his chest, ready to use either end it seemed.

"Nice gun you got there," Mel commented. "I don't recall ever seeing one like it." Except the one he took off the dead soldier in his barn, he recalled.

"It's a Springfield. Fifty-eight caliber. It'll put a hole in a man you could pass a hedge apple through."

"Easy to load?"

"You ain't never seen one of these?" the soldier asked with some surprise. "It fires a paper cartridge with the bullet and powder already in it." He fished a cartridge out of a leather box on his belt and handed it over for Mel to inspect.

"Sure beats a lot of the guns I seen around this camp," Mel noted.

"Gives a man an edge," the soldier agreed. "But we ain't got many of them. I took this un off a fellow who didn't need it no more after our last skirmish."

Mel returned the cartridge, then explained to the soldier, "I thought I might get my blanket and pillow out of my cabin so I could bed down someplace tonight."

"So you're the landowner?"

"I am."

"You still can't go in, not while Colonel Mayfield has his field headquarters set up inside."

Mel wasn't sure what a field headquarters was, but he thought his little cabin must be ill-suited for anything with such a high-toned description. "Then how about calling that other fellow out for me," Mel suggested. "His name is Elliott. Tell him what I need."

The guard considered the request, then told Mel, "I'll see if the major wants to talk to you. Stay here."

A few minutes later Elliott came out carrying the blanket and pillow. "I apologize again for the inconvenience, Mr. Carroll," he said.

"All of this left inconvenient way behind two minutes after you rode into my yard," Mel told him. "It'll take me five years to fix what you fellows tore up in one day."

"A lot worse is likely to happen before this is over," the major warned. "I'm trying to convince the colonel to let you leave. If he does, stay away for at least a week, maybe two. We can't guarantee your safety, not even from our own men."

"Nobody asked you to guarantee nothing," Mel pointed out. "And I'm not leaving unless you run me off."

"Have it your way then, Mr. Carroll. But if you do stay, for heaven's sake don't stir up any trouble. Colonel Mayfield's a stern old bird, and he doesn't tolerate any resistance from the civilian population, especially now that we've crossed the line up into Missouri. He calls it hostile territory. He had the mayor back in Palestine shot two days ago because he tried to stop our quartermaster from requisitioning food and supplies from his general store."

"They shot Merriweather Riggs?" Mel said. "Well, he probably deserved it. I never could stand that swelled-up little crook."

"But that was only the start of it," Elliott said. "The colonel's blood was up by then, so after we emptied the store, he had it burned. Half the town caught fire before it was all over."

"Guess I'll make it a point to steer clear of him, then."

"But you still don't want to leave?" Elliott asked.

"Not just yet."

The major seemed a little exasperated by Mel's stubbornness. "All right then, the least I can do is offer you a billet in one of the officer tents."

"I'm not sure what a billet is, but I already have a place in mind to bed down." The major handed him the bedding and started to turn away, but Mel stopped him with a question. "How'd you boys enjoy Miss Belle?" When Elliott looked puzzled, he added, "The cow I was butchering."

Elliott managed a tired grin. "I haven't had steak that tasty since we left West Helena three months ago."

It was no surprise to find the family root cellar at the edge of the woods stripped of everything edible or otherwise useful. Mel felt around until he located the candle stub and matches he kept in a tobacco tin on a wooden beam above the door. In the faint, flickering light, he made his bed on the low frame cot along one wall of the eight-by-eight space. Closing the door partway, he blew the candle out and laid his tired body down.

In the darkness, old memories came to him. When he was a child his family had spent many nights out here, feeling safe and content when storms thundered and raged outside. Mother would sing hymns or read to them by lamplight about the Savior's life and teachings. Sometimes Daddy would spin yarns about his Indian fighting days, or talk about his family back home in Virginia. The shelter was dug five feet into the ground, with two feet of dirt on top of the layers of logs that formed the roof. Inside the root cellar it was always cooler than the outside air, making it ideal for food storage. By late fall, the shelter was so full of laid-by fruits, vegetables and other preserved foods that they could barely squeeze in and find a place to sleep when bad weather came.

Mel smiled in the dark about the whippings he took for sneaking down here and sampling the preserves and jellies mother had put up for the winter. When he grew older, his target was more likely to be the hard cider, muscadine wine, or corn liquor Daddy stored there.

When he was a boy, those times only seemed like an ordinary part of life. But now, thinking back, there seemed to be something special about those days that he hardly understood. He couldn't leave. Facing whatever was about to take place here wouldn't be as hard as skulking off somewhere and not knowing what was happening to his farm.

CHAPTER THREE

Mel was jolted awake as the walls and ground shivered and quaked all around him and an earsplitting roar tumbled in through the half-open door. Dirt and pebbles from the log roof above showered thickly down on him. His first thought was that it was an earthquake, which wasn't unheard of in these parts. He pictured the roof collapsing on him, crushing him to death, or worse, burying him alive. There were five terrifying rumbles in close succession, then silence.

He tumbled off the cot and out the doorway, scrambling desperately up the steep wooden steps into the open air. No more than ten feet away, the crews of the five cannons positioned above the root cellar were shocked by the appearance of a frantic man who seemed to literally spring from the ground beneath them.

"You could warn a man before you cut loose with a racket like that!" Mel stormed at them.

"Hell, we didn't know nobody was down there," one of the crew laughed. He was holding a long pole with something that looked like a sheepskin brush tied around one end. "I thought we'd woke the dead with that first salvo."

The fifteen or so men manning the big guns all began to laugh, and seeing the humor in it, Mel did too. He had seen the cannons up there last night, but had no idea that they'd start firing them so early. But now he realized that if he was still here and still alive when the sun set tonight, he'd have to think about finding someplace else to sleep.

"Has the fight started already?" Mel asked. The wind was pushing the black pall of smoke from the cannons to the northeast, down into the valley beyond, but he saw no sign of attacking soldiers in that direction.

"Naw, we're calibrating the range," one of the men explained. "When the real fight breaks out, you'll know about it soon enough."

The sun hadn't even risen far enough to start leaking through the treetops to the east, but already the camp was awake and active. Down in the valley the smoke rose from hundreds of breakfast fires, and some of the men were already filing off to finish their work on the earthen barricades on the western and northern portions of the farm.

Last night Mel had considered staying down in the root cellar while they settled things up above him, but this morning he saw that was an impractical plan. Not only was it bound to get impossibly noisy down there, but there were also other normal needs like food, water, and a morning constitutional that had to be taken care of.

The surly little town-burning colonel was up and about already too, surveying the completion of the fortifications on the crest of the hill overlooking White Tail Valley. They looked like they would serve their purpose well, Mel thought. The soldiers could stand in a three-foot ditch behind a long pile of dirt and logs that was raised high enough to lay a long gun across. They could duck down out of the line of fire to reload, then rise back up and take their shot without exposing anything more than their head and shoulders.

The colonel's crew, including Major Elliott, stayed in tow as he strolled back and forth. Every few seconds he would pause, point off in one direction or another, and give somebody an order. The whole thing would probably have come together just as well without him, but some men seemed born to want to tell everybody else what to do.

Mel walked over to the front of the cabin and washed his face and hands at the pump. Outside the cluster of tents nearby he spotted a pot suspended with an iron tripod over a dying fire. No one was around, so he went over and took a look. The pot contained some kind of hash made with potatoes, onions, and shredded beef, all his he felt sure. He found a plate nearby and dipped some of the food out of the pot, then claimed a hunk of half-eaten cornbread from another abandoned plate. Coffee was all this breakfast needed, but the large, smoke-blackened coffeepot in the edge of the fire was empty. Instead he washed his meal down with fresh water from the pump.

Down the hill in the cornfield to the south, the long dirt berm they had thrown up yesterday was crawling with armed men. The cannons covering that approach were perched on the hillside below the barn. The whole scene in the valley was blanketed by a shadowy ground fog that Mel knew would not burn off until the sun cleared the treetops to the east.

Ordinarily the dissolution of the morning fog down in the cornfield would signal that it was time to round up Doc and harness him to the plow. But not today, and probably not for a long time to come.

As he was finishing his breakfast the cannons at the barricade behind the house rumbled out again, and Mel headed back up that way to see what they were firing at. This time he walked up close behind the barricade so he could get a better look. Nobody seemed to notice or care.

As in the cornfield, White Tail Valley was blanketed in morn-ing fog. If he was hunting this morning, Mel would already be down there in the edge of the woods, waiting for the deer to leave the woods and begin their morning grazing. But the deer would be far away today. That first blast from the big guns would have already sent them racing away into the deep woods. Mel hoped that they would return to the valley when this lot left because when all this was over, he'd need their meat to survive on for quite a spell.

The colonel paced by behind him, still barking orders at his underlings. ". . . and tell the platoon leaders to keep reminding the men not to fire until the order is given. Too many of these men are still green recruits, and they haven't developed any battle discipline yet. I believe they'll feint from the north, up this valley, to make us concentrate our forces on this side. Then the main attack will be from the west. They'll want to take the road, and will probably be willing to pay a high price for it. But it's still all guesswork. I'm blind without any field intelligence to help me plan. Damn that idiot Hess all to hell. He must have gotten his fool self captured or killed at the exact time that I need him most."

Dead and buried, Mel thought, but not in the kind of grave a man was likely to pick for himself.

Far down the valley he spotted men moving cautiously toward them. With the bottom halves of their bodies hidden in the thick ground fog, they drifted forward like eerie specters floating on a feathery cloud. There weren't many of them, two dozen maybe, and they were scattered out. As Mel watched their approach, Major Elliott came over and stood beside him.

"They're not sending out many men if they aim to start this thing," Mel said.

"Those are skirmishers," Elliott explained. "Their job is to come close enough to get an idea of our strength and defenses." Three of the cannons fired a volley, but the approaching men were still too far away. The exploding balls threw dirt and grass in the air, but killed no one.

"Did they think they could hit any of them with a cannonball? It seems like a waste of iron and powder to me."

Elliott chuckled. "It would be a miracle," he agreed. "We just want to give them something to think about when they start charging up that valley in force. And besides," he added, lowering his voice, "this is the first time the colonel's had a chance to fire his field artillery in battle. He's showing off a bit, I expect."

"I'm thinking maybe that colonel might be as green as some of those recruits he was talking about a minute ago."

"Colonel Mayfield fought in Mexico with Taylor. Claims to have seen plenty of action down there when they took Mexico City."

"He claims that, does he?" Mel grinned.

"There's rumors to the contrary, but none that are repeated too loudly," Elliott said quietly. "In an army, somebody always has to be in charge, and for us, it's him."

Two of the cannons fired, and Mel watched their dark destructive metal balls arc through the air, their fuses sizzling. This time they went over the heads of the distant line of approaching men, bouncing and tumbling along the ground before finally exploding.

"I expect I could hunt for a year with the powder it takes to fire one of those things off one time. It does seem a waste."

"Everywhere an army travels, about all it leaves behind is waste of one kind or another."

"Looking around my farm, I'm bound to agree with you," Mel said. "But what are you Arkansas boys doing away off up here in Missouri anyway, Major?"

"We're bound to keep those Missourians from advancing on down into Arkansas," Elliott tried to explain. "So we're marching up here to meet them."

"So if everybody stayed home, there wouldn't be any fighting, would there? Or am I only a big dumb hillbilly who doesn't understand anything?"

Elliott gave Mel a curious look. "The fact is, Mr. Carroll, I really don't have a good answer to either one of those questions. All I know for sure is, here we are, and there they come."

The crackle of gunfire down in the valley interrupted their conversation. Judging by the black plumes of rifle smoke, some of it came from the tree line opposite the approaching men, and some from the skirmishers out in the open valley. A few of the skirmishers toppled down into the ground fog, but the rest moved doggedly forward.

"Before daylight we sent a couple of platoons down into the edge of the woods," Elliott explained, "so they won't come too close to our lines without paying for it."

The crackle of gunfire was brisk for a couple of minutes, then began dying away. The remaining skirmishers began to withdraw, still shooting and reloading as they retraced their progress up the valley.

"I'd give my good leg for two companies of cavalry right now." It was the colonel again, still on the move with his entourage trailing along. "Major Elliott, if you will, sir, rejoin my staff now."

"Yes, sir," Elliott said. Then to Mel he said hurriedly, "Mr. Carroll, I suggest that you find a better place to weather this storm. If you stay here, it might reach a point when you'll either have to fight or die. Maybe both."

"Major Elliott! Stop dawdling!" The colonel was clearly annoyed, and Elliott hurried away to catch up with his leader.

Mel had a couple of options in mind for his own safety, depending on where the attack came from and how the fighting progressed. But for now, things were still quiet. The gunfire down in White Tail Valley had stopped, and the men the colonel had sent down there earlier were now hightailing it back.

Mel saw a man taking the makings out of a pouch, and he sidled over in that direction. For all he knew, it was his own tobacco, rifled from the curing shed behind the barn. The man rolled himself a smoke, then handed the makings to Mel without being asked. Mel rolled one for himself and stuck it over his ear, wishing that he could somehow retrieve his corncob pipe from the cabin. It was damned inconvenient not being able to set foot in his own home.

"I figure we'll have this wrapped up by dinnertime," the man said. He had on a linen shirt with ruffles down the front, and trousers from what had probably been a brown Sunday suit. The clothes had suffered considerably from the long days of marching and harsh camp life.

"You think so?" Mel said.

"Sure, they ain't but a couple of thousand of them. A sergeant told me he heard two officers talking. They said all these Missouri boys was conscripts, and they didn't have no stomach for fighting. Cowards to a man, on the lookout for any excuse to skedaddle. After we give these boys a drubbing, we can probably march all the way to Springfield. Maybe clear up to Independence, if Ol' Persimmon has a mind to take us that far."

"That's a lot of marching," Mel noted.

"It's what armies do, boy. March and fight, march and fight. Hell, I love to march. Once we done fifty miles in one day, and I could have managed another ten or twenty, but the rest of the outfit was tuckered. Say, where's your musket anyway?"

"I don't have one."

"Stole, huh? Well, after the shooting starts, take you one from some dead man, and then have at 'em. I aim to lay my hands on one of them new Spencer carbines before the day's out."

Mel moved on, glad to get shut of the man. It was hardly worth a smoke to have to listen to that nonsense. He took another look down the long sweep of White Tail Valley, and suddenly they were there. They filled the far end of the valley from side to side, hundreds, probably thousands of them—who knew?—walking doggedly forward, rifles and bayonets at the ready. It was a sight he could never have imagined seeing down there in his lovely, lonely, deer hunting territory.

"Here they come, boys!" somebody shouted, but the announcement wasn't needed. For a moment the scene seemed frozen, all eyes fixed in the same direction, all guns pointed down the long valley before them.

A man in front of Mel, leaning forward against the barricade, muttered to his companion, "Look there, Jesse. They're wearing uniforms. I wish we had 'em too. I'd feel more like a real soldier, I expect."

"You can take it up with the gen'ral next time he invites you over for supper," his companion said. "That is, if you're still around to need one after today."

"Well I'd druther be buried in a uniform, too, if it came to that."

Mel knew it was time to move to someplace safer, but he felt funny about it, even though he had no part in this business and didn't even have a weapon in his hands if he did decide to fight.

Down in the valley the men in the blue uniforms kept coming and coming. There were far too many to count, but he had an uneasy feeling that there were more of them than there were in this bunch up here on his hillside. Without warning the five cannons rumbled out their angry challenge, and down the valley the rounds cut their bloody swaths through the advancing soldiers. But they still kept coming.

Mel turned away and started back toward the enormous mulberry tree where he had decided to weather this thing out.

"You, stop! Get back on line, soldier, before I put a ball of lead between those yella shoulder blades." The voice was harshly confident, and Mel could tell its owner was perfectly willing to do what he said. He turned and saw a man striding toward him. He held a cocked revolver in one hand, and the other rested on the hilt of his sheathed sword. His eyes were furious, his face red as a plum. He wore a complete gray uniform, but instead of the gold on his shoulders, there were stripes on his sleeves.

"Where's your weapon, soldier? Thrown it down already, have you, and the battle not even started yet? I seen yella cowards before, but I never seen . . ."

"Don't call me that, mister," Mel bristled. "This isn't my fight is all."

"I'm about to make it your fight," the man stormed. "Mister!"

Mel stood still, thinking that he could probably take that revolver away from him if he came a little bit closer. But then what?

"Sergeant Boone," a voice called out from nearby.

"Sir?" the sergeant said, keeping his eyes on Mel. He seemed to recognize Major Elliott's voice.

"Holster that weapon, Sergeant, and return to your men," Elliott ordered.

"But, sir, this man . . ."

"That man is a civilian, and he's moving to safety, as I instructed him to do."

The red-faced sergeant glared at Mel a moment more, not able to let go of his anger so easily, but no longer sure what to do with it. Reluctantly he lowered the hammer of his revolver with his thumb and turned back toward the real fight.

Mel thought he should thank Elliott, but the major had turned away too. The enemy was too near now for niceties.

Years had passed since he'd last climbed the old mulberry tree, but his hands and feet remembered the way up into it as if he'd last climbed it only the week before. It was an ideal boy-climbing tree because the limbs were well spaced and stretched far out from the trunk. From near the top he remembered seeing much farther down White Tail Valley than anyone could possibly see from the ground. To the east it seemed like he could see halfway to town, and to the south and west, beyond his cornfield and pasture, the rolling hills and thick virgin forests seemed to stretch to the edge of the world.

To a ten-year-old-boy it was a wondrous, liberating thing to be at the top of a tall tree on top of a high hill. A boy would do it for the pure happiness of the doing of it. But to persuade a grown man to make the climb, it took something a lot more curious and important, like the chance to watch hundreds of men fighting and killing each other to decide who would control a little chunk of ground out in the middle of nowhere.

The shooting and the yelling down below started about then. When the thick mobs of advancing men in the valley reached the bottom of the long hill leading up to the barricade, they all started running and screaming wild, primitive noises at the top of their lungs like crazy people. As the firing from both sides intensified, a thick haze of powder smoke began to blur the battlefield, much like the thick dawn fogs that swallowed the hilltop in more peaceful times.

The attackers in front began to fall by the dozens, their battle cries changing to shrieks of pain. The men behind them leaped over their bodies and kept on running. Few even paused to reload their muskets, choosing instead to keep moving as they clumsily rammed home fresh powder and ball. Like a running deer, instinct told them that stopping made them an easier target.

Each time the hilltop cannons fired, the speeding balls cut swaths through the advancing throng, and their final explosions wreaked dreadful carnage. Men were splattered, dismembered, beheaded and mutilated in a shocking variety of ways, like random victims of some terrible vengeance at the very hand of God.

But Mel figured that God didn't have much to do with the slaughter on his farm today. This was the work of fools, carried out with wondrous zeal.

There were casualties behind the barricades too, but not so many. Here and there men fell, some never to move again, and others screaming and clawing at ugly gushing wounds. Mel watched without sympathy as the red-faced sergeant who had confronted him earlier fell to the ground. His body flopped like a hooked fish as blood and brains spilled out of a gaping head wound, and then he lay still, ignored and unattended.

At times the thick gray pall of powder smoke grew so thick that Mel wondered how any of them could keep on fighting, but they seemed to manage, firing blindly into the smoke when no clear targets were in view. Then a breeze would sweep across the hill, clearing the air temporarily, and the fighting would surge with renewed energy.

Through it all, the sour little colonel, the one they called Ol' Persimmon, stayed on his feet behind the trench like a willing target. Mel didn't like him one bit, but he knew a man with grit when he saw one. The whole scene had lapsed into pure chaos, but the colonel acted like he was still running things. Above the din of the battle he kept shouting orders to his staff, or at least those who were left, pointing this way and that and sending them rushing away to carry out his commands.

Elliott was still with the colonel, but by now he had a bloody rag tied around his upper arm, and he seemed none too steady on his feet. Loss of blood, or even the sight of his own blood spilled for the first time in any great amount, could make a man woozy.

Down in the cornfield things were exactly opposite of what they were on the hilltop behind the cabin. Hundreds of men were holding steady behind their long dirt berm, but not a shot was fired and not a single enemy soldier was in sight in the broad empty space before them.

Mel wondered what those men down there were thinking and

feeling right now. Was it relief that their lives were not in danger, or were they envious of the ones up here, who were at least doing what they all came here to do? More of the latter, he suspected. For most of them it all had to do with the glory, he thought. But there didn't seem to be much glory in what he'd seen so far.

He wasn't surprised when the attack began to falter and then fail. The front ranks were still a hundred feet from the hilltop, but at that distance they were almost too close to miss, and none could make it any nearer to the barricades. For a short time it was hopelessly confusing out there as the men in back kept moving forward while the ones in front started falling back. Then the whole lot was retreating, some keeping up their fire as they withdrew, and others merely running back to where they started.

The attackers took what wounded they could with them as they moved out of musket range, but many more were left behind. As the next breeze raked away the remnants of smoke from the battlefield, a pathetic scene unveiled. Among the dead were many other men still alive who cried out pitifully for help, or tried to crawl away to safety. But there was little cover to be found, except the mutilated bodies of their comrades.

A few of the riflemen behind the barricades practiced their marksmanship on those sad survivors, which Mel thought was a shameful and unnecessary punishment for men who had so recently shown their own bravery, if not their best judgment, by charging up that hill. The officers finally put a stop to it, labeling it a waste of ball and powder to kill men who were all most likely to die soon anyway.

Soon the defenders began to haul their own dead and wounded up out of the trenches and carry them back from the firing line. There were several dozen of them, but not nearly as many as the other side had lost. The dead were left laying nearby, while the wounded were carried away on canvas stretchers. Mel realized that his smokehouse had been turned into a rough hospital, and before long a chorus of nerve-jangling screams poured out of there. As he watched, Mel saw a disconnected arm fly out the side window, and it was far from the last human limb to be discarded that day.

A large group of men had been waiting idly halfway down the hillside in front of Mel's cabin during the fight. They must be reserves, Mel decided, positioned midway between the cornfield and the hilltop so they could move in either direction if their help was needed. Pretty smart. Now some of them began to pick up their guns and gear from the ground and walk up the hillside to fill the gaps of men who had been shot behind the barricades.

A man standing near the center of the barricade, smoking a pipe and staring down at his distant enemy, suddenly toppled back like a felled tree. A second later, Mel heard the far-off pop of the rifle shot that killed him. Then one of the men over by the cannons folded and fell. Again a rifle report sounded.

"Sharpshooters!" half a dozen voices bellowed out up and down the line. Every few seconds a rifle shot cracked in the trees on both sides of the body-littered hillside, and many effectively reached their marks until everyone was scrambling to hunker down and hide, or to withdraw far enough back down from the barricade to be out of the sights of the hidden marksmen.

If he ever had to be part of something like this, Mel thought, that would be the job for him. He'd have no stomach for charging out in the open straight into a wall of blazing gunfire. But it might be tolerable to lay back and potshot anonymous strangers who couldn't see you to fire back—that was, if he ever had to be part of a lunatic business like this.

A few of the men behind the barricades tried to return fire, but they were firing blindly. There was really nothing to shoot back at except the woods themselves, and what use was that? Besides, it was dangerous to pop up and risk a shot, and for a few it proved fatal.

Then here came the whole bunch again for a second try at it. Far down the valley the thick mob of men in blue uniforms started forward once more, swarming up the valley like hornets boiling out of a torched hive. But the sharpshooters had changed the rules of the game. The men behind the barricades couldn't stand up into position and prepare to fight, and their leaders couldn't march along behind them, shouting orders and inciting them to stop the attack.

Although it cost some of their lives, a few of the braver artillerymen managed to turn the cannons, and soon were pouring fire into the trees where the sharpshooters were hiding. That seemed to discourage the sharpshooters considerably, and then the defenders in the trenches felt safe enough to rise up from their cover to get ready.

The attack up the long open valley progressed much as before. As soon as they came close enough to become reasonable targets, the men in the front ranks began to run forward, screaming like lunatics as they fired wildly toward the barricades.

Watching from his perch on a broad limb of the mulberry tree twenty-five feet above the ground, Mel could only feel a sort of stunned amazement at the blind, dogged courage of these men. Most of them, especially those out front, must know to a dead certainty that they would never make it. But still they came, running toward a place they would never reach, taking the lead ball God put their name on, then falling and dying as their comrades leaped over their body and ran on toward their own ugly end.

They seemed to be ordinary men, much like Mel himself,

and he had to wonder why they had bought into the notion of all this. Why had they come here in such great numbers, and why were they so ready to fight and die to take over a rocky little hilltop farmstead lost out in the middle of these hills?

Why didn't they march around it and keep on their way?

It might be something he could ask the major if he had a chance. But he hadn't seen Elliott since the sharpshooters started firing, and that might not be a good thing. Elliott could be the only ally he had in the middle of all this mess.

Mel felt a tug and a sting on his upper arm. He looked down and was surprised to see a red stain blossoming on his shirt sleeve.

"Dammit!" he muttered, more annoyed than alarmed. The finger-size groove started to smart almost immediately, and blood began to gather and flow. The bone wasn't hit and he still had use of his arm, but blood was steaming down his arm and dripping off his fingers. He knew he had to do something about it, but there wasn't much he could do up here in the tree.

He climbed down and headed for the cabin, which was the only place he knew where he could find what he needed. He was surprised to find it empty. They had pushed most of his handmade furnishings back out of the way, leaving only his table sitting in the middle of the room, covered with maps and other papers. Other than being rearranged, everything seemed to be about as he had left it.

He took his mother's sewing kit from the shelf where it had been kept all his life, sat down on his cot, and quickly sewed the wound closed with heavy thread. Living alone, a man had to be willing to tend to his own inevitable wounds, and he had patched up worse than this. You learned to put the pain aside when something like this had to be done. He splashed some whiskey from daddy's clay jug on the wound, then wrapped it tight with cheesecloth. Then he poured another couple of splashes of the whiskey down his throat.

Mel was surprised to spot his shotgun by the front door, right where he left it yesterday when all this craziness started. He took it with him when he went out, along with powder and shot. He also grabbed a chunk of bread about the size of a brick, and nearly as hard. On the porch he retrieved his canteen from a nail on the front wall, filled it at the pump, and returned to the mulberry tree.

It was early afternoon now, and judging by the diminishing gunfire, Mel realized that the second attack must also have failed. Back up in his perch in the tree, Mel doused a corner of the brick of bread with water and gnawed at it for a while. The post-battle activities started again below him. This time they rotated some fresh soldiers up from the cornfield where things had been quiet all day, and sent the men who had been in the fight down the hill to eat and rest.

By late afternoon everything seemed to be settling down. Under white flags, several mule-drawn wagons came up the length of White Tail Valley and teams of men gathered up their scattered dead.

That pleased Mel. He didn't like the idea of all those men laying out there to bloat and stink. Any man who died as well as these men had shouldn't have to end up a feast for the wolves, coyotes, bears, and buzzards that lived in these parts. Plus, he had turned his hogs loose the day before, and he knew a hog wasn't too proud to eat a dead man if he had a chance.

The army occupying Mel's farm chose a spot down the hill and across the road to dig graves for their dead. It was better than burying them in the cornfield, as far as Mel was concerned. He had a hard time with the notion of running his plowshare over graves, or eating corn nourished with the flesh and bones of dead men. It might not hurt him, but there was something downright eerie about the prospect.

What happened next at the edge of the battlefield out beyond the hilltop barricade was completely unexpected. Down in White Tail Valley, after most of the dead men had been stacked up in the wagon beds, some of the men assigned to that grisly work began to stray on up toward the barricade. Though most were unarmed, they ventured up within easy musket shot of the men they had been fighting not long before.

But nobody on this side readied their weapon or even seemed surprised by their approach. Soon men from both sides began to congregate in small groups out on the battlefield. They shared tobacco, swapped small items back and forth, and chatter calmly like neighbors meeting along the road.

Mel's curiosity grew. On impulse he lodged his shotgun in a niche between two branches and climbed down to the ground. Soon he was across the barricade and walking toward two men nearby. One wore a blue uniform, now torn and filthy, and the other had on an odd little gray cap and coarse, sturdy work clothes much like Mel's own. Without his asking, the man in the cap handed Mel a small bag of tobacco and a corner of newspaper. Mel tore off a piece of paper and began rolling a smoke.

"We been boiling the same coffee grounds three or four days running," the gray cap man said, "till it got so it wouldn't hardly color the water no more. And now we got nothing."

"Wish I'd known," the man in blue said. "I got coffee back at camp I'd gladly swap for a little of that smoking tobacco. Our supply was in a freight wagon that got burnt up two days ago in a fight west of here. Back home I've got a curing barn full of the stuff, but it don't do me no good away back up in Mirabel."

Mel lit his smoke from one of theirs. The smoke from the burning newsprint stung his nose, but the tobacco was like manna. "How far west was that other fight?" he asked the man in the blue uniform.

"Ten, maybe twelve miles. It was at a little farm place about like this one."

"At the Adderly farm?" Mel asked. The Adderly family were his neighbors, and friends of a sort. It was Rochelle's family. The distance and direction were about right.

"I don't know whose place it was," the man admitted, "but I can tell you that there wasn't much left of it after we finished fighting you fellows for it."

"I'm not in the fight," Mel told him. "This is my farm here. It's the Carroll place, and I'm Melvin Carroll, in case anybody down the road asks about me. Tell them you saw me here, still alive."

"Well, best of luck with it, Mr. Carroll," the man said. "I hope your farm's in better shape than that other one when this is over."

"You mean it's not over yet?" Mel asked. It didn't make sense. Why would these men come out here, casual as you please, if they only intended to go back to their own sides and start shooting again?

"Over?" the man in blue chuckled. "Not likely. Not since our batteries have caught up to us." He pointed over his shoulder with a thumb. Down in the valley, maybe a half mile away, crews were positioning a new row of cannons.

Chapter Four

At dusk, after the fighting was definitely stopped for the day, Mel wandered around his farm to take stock of things. Details of already exhausted soldiers were at work in several places strengthening the defenses they'd built the day before. The colonel and his staff were settled back in the cabin, poking at their maps and doing whatever else they did to make themselves feel important.

He made a wide loop around the smokehouse where the grim hospital of sorts had been set up. The ground outside was cluttered with dozens of moaning, bawling, bloody, wounded men. A few attendants wandered among them, passing out water and food to the ones that were in any shape to accept it. But for the most part the wounded men just lay there, some on blankets and others on the bare, stony ground, suffering without relief, waiting to survive or die, as the Lord saw fit. The pile of legs, arms and other unidentified human gore outside the window was nearly waist high, abuzz with hordes of hungry flies.

As Mel approached, a barn rat scurried away into the shadows, a gruesome prize in its mouth. According to God's great plan of how things were supposed to work, not much ever really went to waste, even at a time like this.

But Mel couldn't see himself ever smoking another ham in this building. He'd have to tear it down, unless these soldiers did it for him during the fight.

The stench around the smokehouse was awful as wounds

began to fester, stumps of severed limbs began to rot, and men who had no other choice emptied their bellies, bowels and bladders where they lay. Evidence that operations were still going on in the lamp-lit interior of the smokehouse came in the form of a man's arm, severed at the elbow, tossed out the window. The pile was mostly arms, given the circumstance of the fight.

Mel hoped that someone would take the time to bury all that mess because he dreaded the thought of dealing with it after they pulled out.

The barn looked curious, with most of the outside planks pulled off as high as a man could reach. Much of that lumber was used in the construction of the defenses. The skeleton of the building looked worth saving, but it would take a lot of work. The inside of the barn was stripped bare. Feed, hay, tools and tack—all of it was gone.

There were no animals anywhere—not a chicken, duck, cow, pig or mule—except for the horses and mules the soldiers brought with them. Mel was most concerned over the whereabouts of his mule, Doc. He had turned Doc loose and watched him head for the woods. But that didn't mean Doc hadn't wandered back, or maybe just kept going to get away from the ruckus. There was no predicting what a mule might do.

Doc might be the single most important possession he would have when all this was over and he started putting things back in order. Doc was a strong healthy animal, still fairly young, and had more sense than most mules did. Although Mel used him for transportation and for most of the heavy pulling and lifting around the farm, his single most vital role was pulling a plow.

Without Doc, Mel couldn't hope to put even part of a corn crop back in in the ground, and without a crop, it would be a hard, hungry winter.

As full darkness settled in, he wandered down the hillside to the camp at the eastern edge of the cornfield, guided by the dim light of dozens of small campfires. The men were more subdued than they were the night before. They stared hollow-eyed and reflective at their metal plates of food, kicked listlessly at their tiny fires, or mumbled empty conversation with their comrades.

For many of them it was probably their first experience with this kind of thing, and Mel figured it wasn't at all what they expected. They probably thought they would end the day's fight all full of pride and righteousness. But for most, the aftermath probably had more to do with remembering the gut-scrambling fear they'd felt when the gunfire was at its worst and death was all around. And there was bound to be some shame and disgust mixed in as well.

War was absolutely real to them now. They were wondering if, after tomorrow, they would be laying outside the smokehouse, bleeding and festering and trying to bear the pain, or laid out down the hill alongside the many other corpses ready for bury-ing.

If tomorrow was anything like today, Mel thought, a lot more of them would end up in one place or the other. He didn't try to talk to any of them, but headed instead to the chow line over by the road.

"Well looka here," the large sweaty cook said, recognizing Mel. "So you stuck around through all that shooting, didja? Must have been my cooking that kept you close by."

"Believe that if you want to," Mel told him. "But the fact is, I've got no place else to go. What's in the pot tonight?"

"We cleaned you out last night, so now we're back to eating what we brought with us." The cook scraped some other man's leavings out of a dented metal plate onto the ground, then filled it with a big ladle from the huge iron pot. "Salt pork, cabbage and potatoes," he said.

"I've had worse," Mel said.

"Don't be so sure of that until you try it," the cook laughed. After this long day of fighting and death, he seemed to be the only one in camp who still enjoyed his work.

Mel carried his plate and spoon over to the patch of ground beside the road that somebody had decided to turn into a graveyard. Long mounds of dirt marked the spot where many of the day's casualties had already been buried side-by-side in shallow trenches. A crew was digging another trench while a score or more of its future occupants were laid out on the ground nearby, waiting patiently for eternity.

In the flickering light of the kerosene lamps that dimly lit the area, Mel stood eating his dinner and looking at the dead men. Their wounds were varied and most were grisly examples of the many ways that a little lead ball could steal a man's life away. One man had a severed leg laying across his chest, and despite the oddity, Mel decided that he approved of that. If it was him, he'd want to be buried with all his parts, even if some of them weren't attached anymore.

It was curious, he thought, that when you looked at a dead man, it was hard to believe that this thing had ever been alive, walking, talking, eating, sleeping, thinking. Daddy had told him it was because the spark was gone—the soul.

Mel guessed he was right. Three years back when he had nursed his father through six long, pain-filled weeks of dying, every day had been a tribulation to both of them. It was horrible watching what the old man suffered through, and more than once he had been tempted to end it for him. But he kept reminding himself that God was at work here, and he would end it in his own time.

Then one day when he woke from one of those deep, troubled naps that passed for rest back then, he realized the room was still. No more gasps of breath into old worn-out lungs, no more moans and sobs of pain, no more broken, delirious conversations with a wife already dead for so long.

Mel knew he was alone in the cabin, although Daddy's body still lay only a few feet away. The father he had loved, learned from, fought with, and tenderly nursed in his last days, was gone. And what was left cooling, stinking and still on the cot was just the useless leftovers, needing only to be dressed up, read over, and put into the ground.

It was the same for these men here. Whatever they had been before, sons, husbands, fathers, fine men or scoundrels, Holy Rollers or heathens, didn't make much difference tonight. The meat and bone all went into the same trench.

After eating, Mel wandered back up the toward the cabin. He talked a cook out of a tin cup of coffee, then sat on a big rock to drink it.

He was still having trouble believing what had become of his simple life and his simple little farm since that morning only three days before when those three men rode into his yard and ended up shooting Belle. He wondered how Daddy would have dealt with all this mess and disruption. Knowing how that tough old frontiersman was, he probably would have raised enough of a ruckus to get himself shot or hung, or at least tied, gagged, and put out of the way somewhere until it was time for this bunch to pull out.

The last mouthful of coffee was full of grounds, and he spit it into the dirt. It was time to turn in. It wasn't that late, but farming folk used to working from can to can't six days a week could generally fall asleep anytime the sun was down and their head hit a pillow.

"Mr. Carroll, I've been looking for you."

Mel recognized the voice and turned to see Major Elliott walking down the hill toward him.

"I wondered if you made it through the fight," Mel said. "I hadn't seen you since midday. I was afraid you caught one."

"I did, early on, but not as bad as some," Elliott said. In the light of a nearby campfire, he looked ten years older than he had that morning. His shoulder wound had bled through its filthy dressing, and the uniform that had been clean and crisp yesterday was a wreck now.

"Is that okay?" Elliott asked, pointing to the cheesecloth around Mel's arm.

"Only a nick," Mel said. "But I'd be obliged if you could take me into my cabin long enough to change the dressing."

"I could ask our doctor to look at it. He was my neighbor back home in Searcy."

"I don't think so," Mel said. "I went by that smokehouse where he's been working, and I don't want anything to do with that place. I figure I might as well burn it down after you're through with it and out of here."

"That might not be soon, Mr. Carroll," Elliott advised. "We've been ordered to hold this position at any cost to deny the enemy the use of that road. We're supposed to have reinforcements moving up tonight or tomorrow. I hope they get here before the enemy has at us again tomorrow."

"Well, I guess I won't be here to see that fight. This afternoon I was talking to a fellow from the other side who came out to pick up the dead. He told me there had been another big fight at another farm over west of here, a bad one, so he said. I think that farm might belong to a neighbor of mine, Ezekiel Adderly. So I guess I'll head over that way at first light tomorrow and check on them."

"I can understand your concern for your neighbors, but heading west is not a good idea," Elliott said soberly. "They're still going at it over there, and you're bound to run into soldiers any way you try, especially by the road. No matter which side you ran into, it probably wouldn't go well for you."

Mel considered the major's warning, then quickly made up

his mind. "I guess I'm bound to try," he said. "There's a girl in that family. Her name is Rochelle, and I need to know what's become of her."

A faint smile came to Elliott's face, and he nodded his head. "I understand. I have a wife and three little ones back home myself, and if I got word that anything might have happened to them . . ."

Mel wasn't sure whether Elliott had choked on his words, or whether he had stopped because he couldn't allow thoughts like those into his head right now.

"But the fact is," the major said, "your chances of surviving the trip would be poor. Our information is spotty because some of our scouts have disappeared. We at least know that General Willard got a shellacking two days ago, but he's not whipped yet. He's still fighting, and those northern boys are still hot after him. If you start west right now, you'll be heading into a hornet's nest."

Mel didn't say anything, but he was thinking of the back-country trails and valleys he might follow to the Adderly place. The road might be faster and easier, but it wasn't the only route to where he wanted to go.

"But there's another reason why we can't let you leave just yet," Elliott said. "We need your help here."

"No, sir, I won't take sides in this," Mel said firmly. "I don't even know what it's all about, but I have an idea that if I did pick a side, it wouldn't be yours."

"That might be, Mr. Carroll, but I'm afraid you don't have a choice."

"A man's always got choices," Mel said. "Even when none of them are any damn good."

"Two weeks ago in a little town called Jefferson," Elliott said, "a man named Goings refused to accept an on-demand note for his horses and mules. He told Colonel Mayfield it was cash or no deal. A few minutes later, when they couldn't come to terms, the colonel had Goings taken out into the street and shot. This is a mean struggle we're in, Mr. Carroll, and life is cheap. I'd hate to see you lose yours standing up for something that's not worth the price you'll have to pay."

Mel said nothing. What was there to say?

"We won't ask you to fight," Elliott said. "We need your help putting some men in place in those woods down along the valley. Those sharpshooters worked us over pretty good yesterday, and we'd like to make sure that doesn't happen again tomorrow when the fight starts to heat up."

Mel considered that. It didn't seem worth putting his life on the line to say no. If things started going bad, he could always lose the men he was guiding, and then he'd be on his own in his home woods.

"There are some trails Daddy and I used when we deer hunted," he told Elliott. "We liked to be at the stand at first light when the deer strayed out into the valley to feed."

"Do they pass by where those sharpshooters were yesterday?"

"Close enough. I could lead your boys right down into the belly of the beast if you had a mind."

"Something tells me we might already be there," the major said tiredly.

CHAPTER FIVE

Mel retrieved his shotgun before they left, and no one objected. There were about twenty men in the group he was to lead, grim-faced and quiet, knowing what a risky excursion this would be. They'd be squared off against expert marksmen with better weapons than theirs, in the dark on unknown ground, and once the day's fighting started, they'd be out there on their own between the two armies.

Major Elliott told him that all the men in the party were volunteers. Mel didn't bother to point out that it wasn't exactly true. He hadn't volunteered.

At least they had been able to get a few hours of sleep before the moon came up. Mel guessed that early dawn was still about two hours off, plenty of time to move down through the woods to the area where the snipers had set up yesterday.

He led the men into the woods toward what he and Daddy called the Dogleg Trail, which followed the meandering downhill path of a creek northeast at first, then after a sharp crook, back toward White Tail Valley. It was an ancient trail, probably used by game and Indians centuries before the first white man found his way into these parts. Mel chose it over a more direct route because it was easy to follow even in the faint speckled moonlight.

He kept the pace easy to keep the noise down, but from time to time he still heard the men in the line behind him stumbling around in the dark, falling occasionally and cursing under their breath.

The man in charge was a young lieutenant named Turnipseed, which was a hell of a name for a man so small, spindly and downright irritating to have to carry around, Mel thought. Mel didn't like him from the start, but then he really didn't need to. After tonight he was pretty sure they would never meet up again on this earth, and he figured he could put up with even this high-toned little jackass for a few hours if it meant putting this job behind him.

The lieutenant repeatedly demanded reassurances from Mel that they were on the right track and that they would get there on time. Despite Mel's warnings to keep quiet, Turnipseed kept reprimanding his men in harsh whispers for one small foul-up or another. The others seemed to barely tolerate him because he had the rank, and not because any of them felt any true respect for him.

Mel stopped the group every few minutes to let the woods go quiet around them. The worst outcome he could think of would be to stumble onto a group of enemy soldiers unawares, and him right up front with no choice but to fight for his life. During each pause he surveyed the woods around them, seeking any sight, sound or smell that wasn't part of the native forest. Turnipseed was impatient with the stops, clearly eager to reach their destination and start shooting at somebody.

When they had followed the faint pathway northwest for long enough, Mel led them off the trail, moving due west now, toward the area where the snipers had been yesterday. Even in the near dark, Mel could move quietly, but some of the men behind him weren't as skilled. At last he paused the group again and knelt to have a whispered conference with Lieutenant Turnipseed.

"The woods end about a hundred yards west of here," Mel

explained, pointing off in the darkness. "We'd best stop here and wait for better light before we move in closer. If there's anybody up there already, it'll only take one of these men stumbling over a root and falling down to let them know we're close by."

"My orders are to proceed to the edge of the valley under cover of darkness," Turnipseed said, "and take up position to ambuscade the enemy sharpshooters when they arrive." He seemed determined to look, sound and act like a soldier, even if he was only a scarecrow kid.

"That's some dandy orders," Mel said, "as long as you're certain they didn't get here before you did. But what if they're already there, up in the trees someplace with those long rifles of theirs, and one of these here clubfooted men steps in a rabbit hole or trips over his tallywhacker?"

"We need to be closer," Turnipseed said doggedly. "How can we set up an ambuscade if we stop back here?"

"I understand that you've got orders," Mel said. "But your men aren't exactly slipping through the woods like bobcats, mister. Maybe your orders don't fit this place and time, and you need to make a new plan."

"That ain't how it works in the army," the lieutenant said with annoyance. "When a superior officer gives you an order, you don't change it whenever it suits you."

"Even if it might keep you alive, and those that are with you?"

"No, sir, not even then."

"Then I guess there's a whole lot I don't understand about soldiering," Mel admitted. But he didn't argue any more. If the leader of this bunch didn't know smart advice when it reached out and slapped him, then there was not much Mel could do. Except stay out of it, of course.

Turnipseed turned away from him and sent word down the

line for the men to take a few minutes of rest, and then prepare to move forward.

Mel found a soft patch of moss under a big chestnut tree and settled back to relax. To his way of thinking, his job here was about done. He had led the soldiers to the place they wanted to be. When they moved up to set their trap, or to spring their enemy's trap, he would just sit here and wait for them. Whether they succeeded or failed didn't make a whole lot of difference to him, but he had a notion that he wouldn't be leading nearly as many men back up the hill to his farm as he had led down here.

Despite the purpose, he felt good being in a place where he had passed so many contented hours in his life. The damp predawn air, the complicated mix of fresh forest odors, the sounds of birds and insects—all conspired to stir old feelings and memories.

Daddy started taking him hunting when he was so little that raising a rifle to his shoulder and pulling the trigger taxed his courage and his young abilities to their extremes. He killed his first deer when he was five, with daddy holding the barrel to steady it while Mel peered excitedly down the sights and pulled the trigger. The recoil nearly broke his shoulder, but he made the kill. By eight he was tromping through these woods by himself, kicking rabbits out of the thickets and plinking squirrels out of the hickory trees.

For families like theirs, hunting wasn't for sport. It put meat on the table when otherwise there might not be any. Together he and his father had hunted the deep woods surrounding their home for so long that eventually, with only a few hand signals, and even fewer words, they functioned as a smooth, effective team.

The hunt he remembered best was the last one he and Daddy went out on, before the pain in Daddy's belly controlled his life and he took to bleeding out of places where a man wasn't supposed to bleed. They had set out early on one of those chilly, late fall mornings when the mountain meadows were silver with frost and a layer of ice as thin as satin lay on the surface of the ponds. Both of them carried long guns, and Daddy had his sidearm strapped on. They had butchered a hog a few days before and meat was curing in the smokehouse, so there was no great urgency to bring home food. But still it was wise to salt and cure as much deer jerky as possible in preparation for the long winter months ahead. Some to eat, and extra to give away if the need arose. That was the family rule.

They followed their customary route down Dogleg Trail, and Mel patiently matched his pace to Daddy's slower, painful gait. Daddy was fifty-two that year, which was into old age in these parts where hard work and hard circumstances wore a man out early. The rheumatism in his hips had bothered him for years, and now his knees were starting to fail him. But the real pain, the one that worried them most, the one they never talked about, was deep in his belly.

Daddy was too prideful a man to ever talk about it, or even acknowledge the pain. But Mel noticed it from time to time, and when he did the sadness and dread pricked some raw nerve inside him. Mother had passed on four years earlier at forty-six, suddenly and mercifully while she was hoeing the vegetable garden. But Mel had a feeling that his daddy would not be so lucky.

During that morning hunt, Daddy sat on a log and emptied himself onto the forest floor. When Mel got a glimpse of the coal-black waste, streaked with lines of fresh red blood, he knew something frightening and odious was happening inside the old man's gut.

Mother had passed on her belief to Mel that every day the Lord let a body walk on his earth was a good day. In the Good

Book, she said, God told them not to worry because if he was watching out for every little bird in the forest, wouldn't he take even better care of mankind, his masterpiece? Mel liked that philosophy and had always believed it helped put hard times in perspective. But when a man had blood in his dung, and moaned out in pain in the middle of the night, it made it a lot harder to cling to high-sounding Bible teachings.

That morning when he and Daddy settled into their stand at the edge of White Tail Valley, the first spackling of sunlight was just starting to slant through the trees behind them. The low thick fog that blanketed the open meadow was so delicate that when a bird flew near the ground above it, it stirred and swirled like steam over a boiling pot.

A quarter mile down the valley a dozen or more deer grazed near the tree line on the far side of the valley. The buck was a fine husky animal, a ten or twelve pointer, Mel guessed, although he was too far away to actually count the prongs on his rack.

Mel decided not to try a shot. The big buck was too far away for a sure kill, and he didn't like the idea of wounding a fine animal like that. The valley had plenty of deer, and others would come closer to the stand.

"In my day," Daddy had said, "when my eyes worked a little better . . ."

"I know, old man," Mel teased. "You'd have clipped that big fellow's toenails for him."

"You have a smart mouth on you, boy," Daddy said. "About big enough to put my boot in, I'd say." But he was smiling. He knew how to take a razzing.

Daddy shot an elk that morning, a rare kill in these parts, and a treat for the two men. Cooked right, elk meat was delicious, coarse like beef, and not as gamey as venison. The sleek, proud animal was so large that Mel had to fetch the mule to bring it up to the cabin.

As it turned out, that was Daddy's last hunt, and his last trip down into the woods that bordered the long beautiful valley that he had named when he and Mother first carved out a home here in this wilderness. The pain from the sickness that was gnawing away at his insides soon began to make all his decisions for him, and he passed on that winter.

Settled comfortably on the moss, Mel thought it would be easy enough to drop on off to sleep. But the daylight was arriving, enough so that he could make out the dim shapes of the soldiers stirring around on the forest floor around him.

Soon they would be moving on toward the fight. When that happened, Mel had already decided he'd fade out into the woods until the whole thing was over. He already had a spot in mind, a cane thicket so dense and disorienting that any stranger who wandered into it might spend hours trying to find his way back out again.

The lieutenant gathered his men around him and gave them some final instructions. "When we move out, keep good intervals, stay quiet, and keep a sharp lookout in all directions, even up. If the sharpshooters aren't here yet, we can hunker down and pick them off. And if they are already up in the trees, they'll have their backs to us and they'll make easy targets."

And you for them, Mel thought.

"If they're not in position yet," Turnipseed said, "we'll set up a U-shaped ambuscade and wait for them to move into it. Don't fire until I give the word, then fire at will as fast as you can pull the trigger and reload. The colonel said that any man who comes back with one of them sharpshooter rifles they use will earn himself a quart of whiskey, the real Kentucky sippin' stuff out of his own stock."

Mel was surveying the narrow draw they were in, trying to figure out the best place to hunker down out of sight once the soldiers started moving forward.

"You, farmer!" It took Mel a moment to realize the lieutenant was calling to him.

"I've got a name," Mel said, irritated. "It's Carroll."

"I'll try to remember," Turnipseed said impatiently. "Now, when we move out, I want you on the far right flank. You have a sharp eye and you know these woods, so I need you over the closest to . . ."

"Hold on now. This ain't my fight, mister," Mel said. He was tired of reminding people of that. "You boys are welcome to whale away at each other as long as you want. But when it all starts, it starts without me."

"That's not the way this one shakes out, farmer. We need you with us, and when things start up, you're in it with us."

"What if I say no?"

"Then it'll go hard for you."

Mel saw several men tense, their hands on their rifles, and he realized that this was another choice he would not be allowed to make for himself. He was damned tired of being put in these straits.

The lieutenant spaced his men a few paces apart, facing the valley, and they started slowly forward, looking for any signs of the dreaded sharpshooters ahead. Caution and tension hunched their shoulders like old men, and they gripped their weapons tightly, at the ready. Any time a man's foot snapped a stick or rustled in the damp morning leaves, others glared at him savagely. It is a bad place to be and a god-awful bad plan, Mel thought to himself, and him out here with entirely the wrong kind of gun for the work at hand. He felt nearly bare naked.

Somewhere farther down the valley, the cannons Mel had seen the other army move in yesterday afternoon began to cut loose. They were safe enough here from all that, but it was poor consolation to Mel because he knew that the iron balls would be landing all over his farm at the top of the hill.

Turnipseed had ordered two of his men to stay within easy shot of Mel and keep an eye on him during this advance. Their orders were simple. Shoot him if he tried to hide or run, and shoot him if he wouldn't fight. Mel's order was even more direct. Arm himself with the rifle of the first fallen man he could get to.

Mel heard a bullet slap into the chest of the man to his right in the same instant that a rifle report pierced the morning stillness. As the body sagged onto the damp bed of leaves and moss, Mel threw himself forward and rolled behind the rotting trunk of a downed tree. The other man assigned to watch him was too busy protecting his own body from unwelcomed bullet holes to worry about where Mel was or what he was doing. He found a hiding spot behind the upturned root ball of the same tree Mel was using for protection.

The next few minutes were eerie and unsettling. There was no steady gunfire, just an occasional shot from one place or another up ahead. Once in a while a distant voice called out a location or heralded a hit. Wriggling his body, Mel tried to burrow deeper into the damp leaves and soft, pungent tree rot, hoping that no parts of himself rose high enough above the tree trunk to make a target.

The man killed near Mel was drilled through dead center of his chest, right where the heart was. Mel figured those men in the trees up ahead were probably the best their army had, and though they didn't fire often, they probably had a man, or some part of one, dead in their sights every time they pulled the trigger. It was pure craziness to think that a bunch of men tromping around on the ground under them were any match for their marksmanship, and they had the cover of the leaves and branches to hide their location after they took a shot.

He didn't raise up to look around, but Mel could tell by the sounds around him that there were other casualties among the scattered, pinned-down soldiers he had led down here. Off someplace a man was crying and praying, half mad and desperate, and someplace else another was pleading to his comrades.

"They kilt me, boys! Can't anybody make it over this away and see to me? I'm so sorry, Lena, darling. I'm sorry I come so far after I promised you I wouldn't, and now caught a bullet and died."

Lieutenant Turnipseed seemed to finally find his wits and tried to take command. He called out from wherever he was hiding. "Listen, men! We can't stay hunkered down like this or they'll kill us all!"

"You reckon, Lieutenant?" a muffled voice answered back.

"We've got to charge them, men," Turnipseed called out. "On my command, platoon, we take the fight to these bastards."

Mel looked over at the nearby soldier, who was now burrowed halfway under the fallen tree's root ball. The man was gazing back at him, his eyes full of fear and uncertainty. Every second or so his gaze strayed over to the dead man near them, then back at Mel.

Mel shook his head and hissed in a low whisper, "Don't do it. You'll end up like that fellow if you do."

"Got to," the man whispered back. "Officer's orders."

"Okay, but I ain't," Mel told him. "If you try to make me, I'll kill you myself."

The cannons in the distance were still pounding, and by now the ones on the hilltop at his farm were beginning to answer back. The sharpshooters in the trees ahead were still plinking away, taking their time with each shot. It was the way he and Daddy used to hunt squirrels in these woods, and more often than not, back then and now, it was one shot one kill.

Mel figured the lieutenant was probably trying to put together the courage to order the charge.

And then he found it.

"All right, men, let's shoot them down out of these trees," Turnipseed shouted out. "Let's go!"

There was a lot of yelling, commotion, and gunfire. Mel assumed the soldiers had started their charge, although he didn't rise up to have a look. The man behind the root ball rose to his feet and went running off toward the fight. Soon the forest was filled with the sound of gunfire, and a breeze from the west carried the smoke and the smell of the shooting back toward Mel.

It was as if a thick fog had blown in, and Mel decided that the smoke was the best cover he could hope for. He crawled a few yards to the dead man nearby and gathered up his rifle and paper cartridges. Carrying them and the shotgun would mean extra weight, but he might run into some problem where a second gun was welcome. Then he rose to his feet and hightailed it away from the fighting, back toward the deep woods to the east.

Down in a little draw beyond the creek that bordered Dogleg Trail was a cane thicket as dense and forbidding as a wild blackberry patch, and he headed for that. Ten feet into it, a man could disappear completely, and he needed someplace to hole up and sort things out.

Back behind him the shooting was growing sporadic again. Mel figured that wasn't good news for Turnipseed and his desperate, idiotic charge.

"Hey, slow down," a voice called from behind. "I'm winded and I can't keep up no more."

Mel looked back and saw the man from the root ball clumping along behind him through the smoke. He had lost his rifle somewhere, or threw it down, and he was panting like a dog in July.

"Thought better of it, did you?" Mel asked.

"I never did like that little gandy rooster of a lieutenant," the man huffed, drawing closer. "None of us thought he had good sense. I guess this proves it."

"I'll slow a little, mister," Mel said. "But you'd better keep up if you want to stay with me."

"I will, if my heart don't stop."

When they reached the cane thicket, Mel led the way in. They spooked a deer, which went crashing away through the cane and out the other side. They settled on the ground in the tiny space where the animal had been laying.

Mel's companion was named Trent Giles, and when he caught his breath, his talkative nature soon began to annoy the hell out of Mel. But Mel was still glad he'd brought Giles into the cane hideaway because he had tobacco.

"I thought I might be willing enough to fight until I saw a neighbor of mine from back home go down not ten steps from the place he'd hunkered down. Then I saw another boy that I'd shared mess with all the way up from Arkansas lose a chunk of his head from one of those fifty-caliber bullets. It scared me so bad I wet my britches, and then I turned around and skedaddled. The lieutenant oughtn't to have ordered his men to go out and get themselves slaughtered like that. There was some fine men in that lot. My friends and neighbors."

"Well if there's any such a thing as justice," Mel said, "he's caught one himself by now."

"No one would miss him except maybe his mama. His daddy's a big planter down in the Delta and might of bought himself an officer's commission, but his gout's so bad he cain't hardly walk no more. So he bought his boy a commission instead. Talk is the lieutenant raped a reverend's daughter down in Jonesboro on the way up here, but he convinced the colonel that the lady was willing. And now this turkey shoot. The man can't soldier for squat," Giles said, spitting to the side for emphasis. "Always blaming somebody else for his boneheaded mistakes. And he's big on punishment. The hard kind. I bet if he seen me run off back there and he makes it back hisself, he'll do his best to have me shot. You too, maybe."

"Wouldn't surprise me," Mel said.

"Does that have something to do with why we're up in this cane thicket?"

"If your boys don't win that fight over there," Mel explained, "I figure they'll be backtracking this way before long. I want to let them get on by."

"But if Turnipseed makes it back and reports to the colonel . . . ," Giles said. "If he tells him about how you and me run off . . ."

"Don't go back," Mel suggested. "I'll show you a roundabout way to the post road, and you can start on home to Arkansas."

"I might have run this one time a while ago," Giles bristled, "but I ain't a deserter, nor a coward either. I didn't want to waste my life this morning for nothing, but I've still got plenty of pluck left in me for the real thing. I'm bound to head back up that hill, for my own pride's sake."

"That does change things a bit," Mel said quietly.

Off to the west in White Tail Valley the unexpected roar of hundreds of voices rose up to challenge the din of the cannon fire. The air filled with the distant crackle of gunfire.

"I need to be up there," Giles said with a new sense of urgency. He started to rise, but Mel stopped him with a hand on his shoulder. "Sit tight for a spell," he said. "There'll be fight enough left when you get back. Wait here and let me take a look around."

Picking up the rifle and leaving his shotgun, Mel worked his way out of the cane thicket and found a spot where he could lay down and watch the trail. He didn't have long to wait.

Less than half the soldiers who had set out on the predawn raid now came straggling back. They weren't a military unit anymore, but a collection of bloody, bedraggled, discouraged men. Most were wounded in one way or another, and some supported others the best they could as they stumbled up the trail.

Mel wondered if they had been able to shoot even one enemy sharpshooter down out of those trees. He doubted it.

Turnipseed was with them, but he had left all his cockiness behind somewhere along the trail. He limped along, favoring a bad right leg, holding a blood-soaked bandage against his side. Like Giles he had lost his weapon, but still clutched the little braided leather quirt that he seemed to consider his badge of authority.

Once the lieutenant was patched up and had figured out a way to let the responsibility for the failed raid slide off of him, he'd turn back into the same cocky little bastard, Mel knew. But he didn't have time enough left for that.

Mel stayed hunkered down until the ragged bunch had plodded past where he lay, then tracked their movement up a little rise. When they were about twenty feet from the crest, he cocked the rifle and drew a bead.

It was an easy shot at no more than seventy-five yards, right between the shoulder blades, clean and final. The whipped, miserable survivors didn't even pause to figure out where the shot had come from. They scrambled over the hilltop, leaving yet another corpse behind.

CHAPTER SIX

The fighting was reaching the point of desperate savagery by the time Mel and Giles came out of the trees at the head of Dogleg Trail. Giles wished Mel good luck and rushed toward the faltering defenses overlooking White Tail Valley.

Mel almost turned and headed back into the deep woods. He knew plenty of places where he could hole up until this was over, and with this rifle he had brought back with him, he wouldn't go hungry.

But something kept him from leaving, as surely as if a tether to the farm was tied around his ankle. The farm was nearly destroyed and he couldn't do anything to save the scraps that were left. He still had it in mind to head over to the Adderly place and see how they had fared, but right now a whole attacking army stood in the way of that.

Maybe it was his simple curiosity that kept him here, he thought. He had never seen anything like this before, and couldn't imagine that he ever would again. Maybe it was as simple as wanting to stay around and see how the whole ugly thing ended.

The perch up in the mulberry tree was comfortable and familiar. From there he was able to view a broader picture of how desperate the morning's fighting had become.

His barn was a blazing mound of wreckage, burning so fiercely that Mel could feel the heat of it even where he sat two hundred feet away. The cabin, though not on fire, had a gaping hole on the front side big enough to drive a bull through. The log walls and timber roof, once so sturdy, tight and familiar, tilted at crazy angles. There would be nothing for it, Mel knew, but to knock the whole thing down and start over. The smokehouse was still standing, but he figured it would only be a matter of time before a ball from the cannons down in the valley found it too.

The approaches to the barricades at the head of the valley were carpeted with dead men. Some lay as near as thirty or forty feet, showing how close they had come. In the next attack, or one of the ones after that, they would make it to the barricades, assuming they had the men left to do it with. It was still mid morning, so there was plenty of the day left to cost both sides many more lives.

The defenders behind the barricades were in miserable shape. Now, during a lull in the fighting, they squatted on the ground or leaned against the barricade, trying to gather the strength and resolve for the next round of fighting. They looked like whipped men already, even though they were somehow still holding their ground.

The dead and wounded lay untended where they had fallen. The ones who could struggled to tend to their own bloody wounds and broken bodies, and those that couldn't just lay there bleeding, suffering, and dying.

Down the hill in front of the cabin the reserves were gone. Everybody was in it now, and when a wounded man fell away from the barricade, there would be no one else to step up and take his place.

Down in the cornfield, Mel could see that they had fought off at least one attack there, too. Countless bodies were scattered around the western half of the field beyond the dirt berm they had put up.

Now everyone was waiting for, and no doubt dreading, more

of the same.

Mel spotted Giles, now with his comrades behind the barricade. Most of them had gathered up an assortment of cast-off rifles, and were now checking and loading them. Mel recognized a few of the other men who had followed him down the trail before dawn. Their survival down there this morning might not mean much if another attack was launched against their sparse ranks.

He didn't see any sign that their dead lieutenant might be missed. At this point they didn't need anyone to give them orders. Only one course was left for them. Hold, fight, die.

A couple of officers, bloodied like the rest, still strode the open ground behind the barricades, but Mel couldn't see Elliott or the cranky old colonel, who was the man responsible for this two-day turkey shoot. Both dead, Mel figured, but the only one he could bring himself to feel bad about was Elliott.

Eventually Mel drifted off to sleep with his head tilted back against the thick mulberry trunk and his legs stretched out on a broad limb. His dreams were choppy and broken. Mother calmly chopping weeds in the vegetable patch while the horrible carnage of war raged all around her. Daddy, bent with age and wracked with pain, trying feebly to right the careening cabin walls. Old Justice, half butchered, but still managing to stare up at Mel with those dumb, doleful eyes. Rifle sights settled in the middle of a man's back, and the familiar feel of the grooved trigger as his finger slowly tightens.

The cannons down in the valley opened up unexpectedly, jolting Mel awake. Only two big guns behind the hilltop barricade were still able to answer back. On arrival, some of the cannonballs simply bumped across the ground at amazing speed, destroying everything in their path. Others exploded when they hit, or just before, or just after, hurling up great clouds of dirt, smoke, debris, and human remains, filling the air with deadly chunks and shards of metal. One ragged chunk about the size of an oak leaf lodged in the tree limb directly below Mel's leg, and he dug it free with his knife. It was hot like it had just come from a forge, all sharp points and ragged edges that could rip through human flesh like a hatchet.

Down in White Tail Valley the smoke from the cannons began to drift across the clear ground like odd, unexpected fog. Then, like restless deadly daytime spirits, the lines of men began to emerge from the haze of cannon smoke. Even after all the killing that had gone on before, there were still hundreds of them, in no seeming hurry, spreading like a great blue blight over the valley floor.

Mel could imagine that if he was in that ragged mob down there behind the barricades, it must be a terrifying sight. But still they held instead of running off. He had to give them credit for that.

A cannonball landed almost directly in front of where an officer was standing behind the fighting line and immediately exploded. When the chunks of dirt stopped raining back down and the smoke drifted away, there was nothing left of him. It was like he had simply disappeared, or had never existed at all. But that wasn't it, of course. He was still here, only now he was little chunks of skin, bone, meat and hair, scattered in a twenty-yard radius of where, seconds before, he had stood as a living, breathing man.

Mel figured that was a sight that would return to his mind, awake and asleep, many times in the coming years . . . that, and a lot of other things he had seen here in this gruesome, bloody killing ground that used to be his home.

As before in the previous attacks he'd watched, the men down in the valley began to yell and bolt forward about the time that they drew within range of the men behind the barricades. They were knocked down in droves by the defenders who, at least for these first few minutes, didn't have to pause and reload because each of them had spare long guns within reach.

As before, the attack faltered then failed, but this time the attackers didn't withdraw all the way down the valley. They simply moved back beyond easy rifle shot, leaving a new scattering of dead and wounded men atop the corpses from their previous charge. Some of the retreated soldiers fell flat on the ground to rest, and others knelt alone and in clusters, showing that they didn't intend to have at it again any time soon.

Once again stillness settled over the battlefield. It was so quiet that Mel decided to climb down and get a drink of water while he had the chance. He deliberately avoided looking closely at the cabin as he walked past it to the pump. It was too heartbreaking to think of his family home in such a state. There would be time enough later to consider whether anything could be saved.

While he was at the pump a young soldier limped down the hill carrying two buckets. Mel recognized one of the buckets as his own handiwork, made to carry corn and slops down to the hogs.

The man's soot-glazed features were tight with strain, shock and fear. He had a bullet crease on his scalp above one ear, but hadn't bothered to tend to it. The stream of blood that flowed down his cheeks and neck, into his shirt, was dark and nearly dried. His eyes were flat and expressionless, as if the soul behind them had departed.

Mel worked the pump while the young soldier held one bucket, then the other, under the surging flow of water.

"They killed my daddy," the young man said unexpectedly. "He's laying up there with a hole in his chest you could stick your hand through. So what am I going to write home to Mama? Tell me that."

Mel thought the man must be mistaking him for someone he

knew, or at least a fellow soldier. "Sounds like you should head on home and take care of it in person," he said.

"Nope, can't do that. If I stay here and kill enough of these bastards, maybe I'll get the one that killed my daddy."

"That's a lot of killing, boy," Mel said. "You figger you can kill them all?"

"Just my share, and now Daddy's share."

Heading back to his mulberry tree, Mel decided he could understand the young soldier's gut hatred easily enough. But in a mess like this, he stood as strong a chance of being killed right up there beside his dead daddy as he did in killing his share, whatever that might be. And then who would write home about the two of them?

By the time he reached his perch once again, gunfire was starting up in another direction, down the hill in the vicinity of the cornfield. He climbed one branch higher for a better look, and it didn't take long to figure out that those men down there were about to be in a lot of trouble. But at this point, some of them didn't even seem to realize it yet.

Down there the defenders had built their defenses facing west, across the cornfield and straddling the post road. At the time it made good sense to Mel. If the enemy army was to the west, wouldn't that be the direction they would come from, and wouldn't they spread out and attack once they were close enough? The scattering of bodies across the cornfield, leftovers from this morning's attack down there, was proof enough that the strategy was correct.

After this morning's fight, Mel had realized that any man had to have rocks for brains to attack across that long open field toward armed men hiding behind a long mound of dirt. It was way beyond what any sensible person would consider heroic. Plainly, it was nothing more than a fast, easy way to get shot.

The leader of those men on the other side seemed to have

reached the same conclusion, although it seemed a shame to only see the light after so many had already died. This time the soldiers didn't rush out on another terrifying, bloody race across open ground. Instead they used stealth. A large number of them slipped around in a broad loop to the south, and when they did attack, it was across the cow pasture on the southern side of Mel's farm. That meant that instead of charging head-on against a long, well-protected line of men behind the berm, they hit the line from one end. The dirt berm was of no use to the defenders then, and they were caught completely off guard.

The attackers burst through the line of trees and brush that separated the pasture and the cornfield, made quick work of Mel's split-rail fence, and began the slaughter. Within a couple of minutes clusters of men all over the field were fighting face-to-face, hand-to-hand, and Mel witnessed firsthand how deadly one of those long bayonets at the end of a rifle could be in seasoned hands.

Meanwhile the cannons down in White Tail Valley opened up again, and the troops who had been waiting there started forward with an enthusiastic cheer, as if the battle was won already. And maybe it was, Mel thought. Things didn't look promising for the men who had taken over his farm three days ago. Outnumbered, outgunned and outflanked, he didn't see how they could hold out much longer.

But at least when they were all gone, dead or run off, he could head over to the Adderly place and see how Rochelle and her family had fared. Then when he was satisfied that they were alive and well, he'd come back here and pretty much start over, like his daddy and mother had done in the first place. It would take years of hardship and hard work to rebuild and put things right again. But they'd done it back then, and he could do it now. With any luck, Rochelle might be right there with him through it all.

Mel knew the end was close when he noticed a sprinkling of men turn and bolt as the fighting became unbearable and they started hearing the devil whispering their names. They scattered back through their own camp, then past the wagons, fleeing east down the post road. Others joined them a few at a time, until at last a full-scale rout was under way. Among those who stayed behind, a few surrendered, throwing down their weapons and raising their arms high.

Some others fought on to the death, which wasn't long in coming. That seemed pointless to Mel, although he understood that their blood was up, and it just wasn't in some men to ever give up or turn tail.

When the men at the barricades behind the house realized that their comrades down in the cornfield were whipped and scattering, it came to them how hopeless this whole mess was. Mel could see the panic wash over the thin defensive line as they faced the real possibility of attack from both front and back. At that moment they stopped being an army and turned into a frantic mob of scared, desperate, exhausted men whose only thought was to escape and somehow survive. They threw down weapons and left wounded comrades pleading behind, stampeding down the hillside toward the road that represented their only hope of survival.

As before a few reckless souls stayed behind to fight on, but they didn't hold out long before the waves of enemy soldiers poured over the barricades.

The two attacking groups met and merged at the road, then raced on after their panicked, fleeing enemies. They no longer seemed satisfied by taking the hilltop farm. Now they were determined to wipe out the straggling survivors who had fought to keep them from it.

The sound of scattered gunfire down the road moved farther and farther away. Mel wondered how long the chase would continue before the winners satisfied their appetite for victory. Would they chase their enemies on down to Palestine, or maybe even all the way back into Arkansas? To Mel's thinking that would be just fine. That Arkansas bunch had no business coming up here into Missouri and stirring up this kind of trouble anyway. What was the use in taking over a man's farm and making this kind of mess of it?

Things seemed eerily calm in his vicinity now. No one had yet showed up to attend the wounded, and dead men lay everywhere. Far down White Tail Valley the cannon crews loafed around their silent guns, their duty completed for a time. Except for them, there was no one else in sight who was alive and fit.

Mel decided it was time to climb down and scout around. He hadn't tasted a bite of food since the night before, and the stinging ache in his shoulder reminded him that his wound needed dressing.

Over near the ruins of his cabin he came across the body of the Arkansas colonel who had led this bunch here, or at least what was left of him. One leg and part of an arm were gone, and the rest of him looked like it had been chewed on by wolves. His one remaining dead eye stared up at heaven as if hoping that was the direction his soul was heading. But Mel had his doubts. It didn't seem reasonable that any man responsible for this much death and misery deserved to sit at Jesus's feet.

Mel knelt by the colonel's body and removed the belt that supported his sword, holstered pistol, and cartridge case. They were fine, expensive weapons, and he felt he deserved them after all the trouble this pompous little man had brought into his life. There was little else in the colonel's pockets except a few coins and a letter so soaked in blood that nobody was ever likely to make out what it said.

He wondered in passing what had happened to the major. Elliott had treated him decently through this entire tribulation, and Mel wished him well. He hoped that Elliott had the common sense to take off when the others had, and that somehow he managed to survive the slaughter on down the road. But he would probably never know.

With its crazy tilting walls and gaping holes, the cabin was a sorry mess. But it didn't seem in immediate danger of falling down in the next few minutes, and there were things inside that he needed.

He crawled on hands and knees through the hole that had been the back door and sat up to take a look at the wreckage. Everything inside looked like it had been stirred and battered around by a giant hand. All the familiar things that he used in his everyday life, the furniture, utensils, keepsakes and belongings that made this place a home, lay scattered and damaged. It was heartbreaking, but Mel set his disappointment aside and concentrated on what he needed to do.

Crawling on his belly under a fallen beam, he reached the area of his narrow bed and was able to sit up again. He found the whiskey jug over behind the bed where he left it and took a healthy slug, then another, and then another. It burned in a pleasant, satisfying familiar way going down, and he could feel it starting to relax the tension in his body.

He took off his shirt and gingerly peeled away the crusty bandage that covered his arm wound. It hadn't started to heal yet, and the skin around it was swollen to an angry red. The seepage that started to ooze out was a mixture of blood and milky pus. That wasn't an encouraging sign. Untended, a man could lose an arm from less than this.

He couldn't locate the cheesecloth he had used to dress the wound before, so he tore off a strip of bedsheet and doused it in whiskey. He scrubbed the festering wound until it was raw and painful and oozing healthy dark blood. After a splash of whiskey for his injury and a couple of slugs for his insides, he fashioned a new bandage from more of the bedsheet.

Crawling back to the cooking area of the cabin, he located a few scraps of meat, bread and vegetables scattered on the floor and wolfed them down. A smoke-blackened pot provided some middling sops of gravy, and an overturned bucket with an inch of water remaining helped quench his thirst.

Mel had to chuckle at the thought of what Mother would have said if she'd seen him eating off the floor like a dog. She had always kept a clean, well-mannered household. More than once she'd sent him out to the barn to, as she termed it, "sleep with the other farm animals" when his conduct at the dinner table had crossed her boundaries.

But what use were manners in a fix like this?

A soldier's kit bag he found in a kitchen corner offered a treasure of useful things. On top was a briar pipe with silver trim and a deep, distinctive curve. He had seen the colonel smoking this very same pipe. Mel filled the pipe from a tobacco pouch he found and lit it with an ember from the smoldering fireplace, then settled in to explore his find.

The skinny old man's clothes were useless to Mel because they'd never fit his lanky frame. There was a folding knife, much too small for farm work, but nicely made anyway, with a finely carved bone handle and a keen edge. Carefully wrapped in a felt cloth were a shaving kit, gold-trimmed comb and brush, and a fine-smelling toilet water that Mel thought he might be able to use someday if he ever went courting. There were spare parts for the revolver he'd confiscated, including two extra cylinders and three boxes of cartridges. He found letter-writing materials, a journal, and a small framed tintype of a stiff, drab woman who looked like she was constipated.

Down in the bottom of the kit Mel found a fat leather wallet. He was excited at first to see that it was full of paper money, but most of it proved to be Confederate script that wasn't good for much in Missouri except starting a fire. But there were coins in there too, including some gold, and those had value just about anyplace.

Mel stashed his new bounty behind his bed, figuring not too many men would be willing to crawl in here and plunder around like he had.

The unexpected sound of voices outside startled Mel and kept him frozen in place.

"Just look at the corpses, John. God in heaven, we must have killed half their regiment since the battle started."

"I've never seen worse, sir."

"What made them think they could hold this ground, John? We had them outmanned by two or maybe three to one, and after we brought up the batteries the outcome was never in question."

"Could have been poor leadership, sir. Or maybe sheer bullheadedness. Not many of these Arkansas boys are big on being pushed back the way they've just come."

"Maybe so, but I hate to think that we'll have to kill every blasted one of them to have this thing over with. Good Lord, John, how I'd love to head home to my children and my books and my practice."

"In God's own time, General."

Mel decided it wasn't the best time to crawl out from the wrecked cabin and make his presence known. He might not be able to make these newcomers understand that he didn't belong to the bunch they had defeated, and that he had no part in this fight beyond owning the land they were fighting over. If he crawled out now, with their general so close at hand, he'd be shot straightaway.

"Since all the buildings are down, I suppose we can locate the field hospital in their officers' tents. But I want our wounded moved to the rear as soon as possible. Tell the quartermaster he's to set up headquarters on that patch of ground behind their artillery emplacement."

"Yes, sir."

"Organize a graves detail, a big one, as soon as possible. If we don't get these bodies underground soon this place will smell like hell itself by breakfast."

"What about the prisoners, sir? We'll have two or three hundred, maybe more, when they're all rounded up."

"There's no good place, is there, John? I guess you can circle those wagons out in that field and put them in the center. Place guards all around the outside. We'll try to move them to the rear tomorrow . . . if we're not fighting off a counterattack by then."

"Doesn't seem much risk of that, General. I'd say this bunch is whipped for proper."

"We've still got Willard somewhere to the west of us to worry about. His other regiments are still more or less intact, and his skills in war craft are miles better than whatever fool put together this stand."

Mel could tell by their fading voices that the two men were moving away. And by the growing commotion on all sides, he understood that this new army was quickly settling in. It was a brand new mess, right on the heels of the one just ended.

He stayed in the wreckage of the cabin for the rest of the day, making as little noise as possible, hearing but not able to see the activity around him, berating himself for getting trapped in a spot like this. He should have hightailed it into the woods as soon as he came down from the mulberry tree, or better yet stayed down in the cane thicket this morning after he'd settled up with that piss-ant lieutenant. But how could he have known that as soon as one army was run off the sad wreckage of his farm, another one would settle right down in the same place?

He had never thought of this spot as anything special, but

these men sure seemed to hold it dear, and worth the wasting of many, many men. It was because it controlled both the post road, and the broad open valley to the north, Major Elliott had explained to him. And what was so special about the road and the valley? Armies needed roads and flat open spaces to move, especially in country like this where the hills were steep and the woods were dense.

Mel never got around to asking Elliott the next logical question, which was why one army was hell-bent to move down this particular rocky, rutted mountain road, and why another army was headstrong to make sure they didn't.

To Mel it was all just circles and bloody, destructive nonsense. If it was his call, he would tell them to go around another way.

Not long after dark the noise and activity outside began to lessen. This was an army exhausted by long days of fighting, and though they had won, the battle had taken its toll on them as well.

Hunkered down in the cabin, Mel was so thirsty he felt like he had swallowed dirt. There was nothing in the cabin to drink except the whiskey, which could only satisfy an entirely different kind of thirst, and hardly seemed appealing when his body was crying out for water.

He crawled to the front of the house and took a look out through the jagged hole the cannonball had torn there. The moon was up, the scattered bodies of the dead and wounded were taken away, and the scene was much like it had been when the other army was bivouacked here.

The main difference was the ring of bonfires out in the middle of the cornfield where the prisoners were now guarded by another ring of armed men. The captured men, some clearly wounded, huddled in clusters in the light of the blazing fires, awaiting the dawn and an uncertain future behind enemy lines. Even if a man made it through the fighting all in a whole piece, it still was no Sunday buggy ride being a soldier.

But no one was in sight close around the front of the cabin, and the pump a few yards down the hill called to him like the promise of a sweetheart's kiss. There wouldn't be any better time than this, Mel decided, easing his way out onto a surviving slab of front porch. He stretched his stiff, painful legs and sucked in a great chest full of the fresh night air, feeling better out in the open air again despite the risk. He slithered down off the porch like a snake, then began crawling cautiously down the hill.

The water was sweet and cool, with that faint, familiar taste of metal that the ground put into well water hereabouts. Mel drank his fill, then splashed some on his face and neck to refresh himself and wash away some of the grime. It had been four or five days—he was losing count—since he had been able to wash up properly, or even put on a clean shirt. He could hardly stand his own stink, and the itching in his drawers made him wonder if he was the only creature living in these clothes.

He tried to stay calm when he heard the footsteps approaching from behind. The question ran through his mind whether the truth or some lie would serve him best. As he turned to face the new arrival, he saw the man lower the muzzle of his rifle toward him. He stopped several feet away, clearly suspicious. The bayonet at the end of the barrel looked four feet long from that angle.

"Just sit tight and let's have ourselves a little talk," the man said. The man's face was shadowy with the moon at his back, but his tone of voice was warning enough.

"I'm with graves detail," Mel said. "I came up here to cool down and get away from the stink for a spell. I'm headed back down there now."

"Why ain't you in uniform?"

"Burying's a messy business. I took it off so I wouldn't get dirt and blood all over it, and then have to live with the stink and filth for Lord knows how long. I took these duds off a dead man."

"What's your outfit?"

"C Company." It was a blind shot in the dark.

"Just one problem. The rebs are doing our burying for us," the man said. "Which means you're one of them escaped up to here, or you're a lyin' sack of shit. Which one are you, mister?" There was a new edge to the man's voice and stance that Mel didn't at all like.

"The lying sack of shit one, I s'pose," Mel said, "if I only get two choices. I didn't think you'd believe the truth if I told you."

"Yeah, you're probably right," the soldier said, taking a decisive step forward. "But I'll let somebody else worry about it."

Fortunately for Mel, the sentry decided to use the steel butt plate of the rifle to deal with the situation instead of the long deadly blade at the other end. But Mel didn't feel so lucky when the rifle butt clipped him high on the cheekbone and sprawled him back. He didn't pass out right away, but he was stunned beyond thought or movement, and his head was clogged with pain. The world swirled dark, blurry and confusing above him, and then went away.

The horizon to the east was beginning to glow red and yellow to announce the coming of day when Mel began to reclaim his senses. He was flat on the ground with his arms and legs splayed out awkwardly, his first sensations those of feeling cold and stiff and miserable in the damp predawn. His brain was a fuzzy, painful mess, and he had trouble putting any sensible thoughts together about what had happened to him or where he was. Somewhere nearby men were talking, their voices low and guarded. He smelled wood smoke and meat frying and coffee boiling. The empty, gnawing hunger in his belly did more to bring him back to his senses than anything else.

As he struggled up clumsily onto one elbow, thunder and lightning exploded inside his head. He raised one hand to soothe the pain and discovered a swollen tender wound there, caked with dirt and drying blood.

Some of it started coming back. The big man with the rifle, his stupid ruse, and the payoff for his clumsy lies. But it probably wouldn't have happened much differently for him if he had tried to tell the truth.

He sat up, waiting for the swimming in his head to let up before trying to move again. First he'd find out where that coffee was boiling and try to talk somebody out of a cup. After that . . . well, maybe the coffee was plan enough for now.

There were men all around, some still asleep on the bare ground, and others starting to stir around in the growing light of morning. In his muddled state, it took Mel a while to realize that none of them wore blue uniforms, and not a single man was armed. Then he understood that he was in with the prisoners captured during the fighting the day before. As he had feared, they thought he was part of the army up from Arkansas.

His eyes fell on a man squatting a dozen feet away, watching him with something like a satisfied look on his face.

"Glad to see you're still amongst us," the man said. "You looked pretty bunged up when they drug you in last night."

"I feel like I've been mule kicked in the head," Mel admitted.

"Well at least you woke up this morning, which is a lot more than I can say for some of these fellows, who won't be waking up today or any other day." His arm swept the scattered bodies around them, and some of them did indeed look dead. "A fellow was about to take your boots when they brung you last night," the man said, "but when he saw you was still breathing, he let you alone."

"I'm grateful to him for that, but I feel most near dead right now."

Mel was beginning to get his bearings. They were in his lower field near the earthen berm the other army had thrown up. The ring of fires he had seen last night were burned down to smoking ashes now, but the ring of blue-uniformed guards, with a ring of wagons behind them, were still there. Nothing remained of the thriving cornfield that had been here a few days before. After all the tromping and digging and fighting and dying, not one of the young corn shoots that he had been so proud of appeared to have survived.

"I'd offer to help you tend that bang on the side of your head, but they haven't give us water but once since noon yesterday, and not enough then."

"It's fine for now," Mel said, struggling to his feet. He was surprised by his own unsteadiness. It was like a Sunday morning after hitting the jug too hard on a Saturday night. "I've got to straighten something out with these bluecoats. I don't belong here. I'm not in this fight."

"Ain't none of us in it no more, seems like."

"I never was, though. This is my land. I live here. Your side understood that and let me be, so they should too."

"So you're the one, huh? I never seed you myself, but I heard a couple of fellows, hardscrabble farmers theirselves, talking about what a shame it was what we were doing to your place."

"I didn't think it could get no worse," Mel agreed. "But now it has."

As Mel started away, the man called a piece of advice after him. "Don't cross past that circle of fires from last night. Learn that lesson from some other fellows that tried and caught a bullet for their boldness."

As Mel neared the edge of the circle, two of the guards noticed his approach and casually swung their rifle muzzles in his direction. They shared a chuckle about something, and Mel wondered if they were joking about who got to shoot him, or maybe what button to aim for, if he came too close. He stopped a pace short of no-man's-land and said, "I need to talk to somebody. A mistake's been made."

"Yeah, and you boys made it, thinking you could hold your line against the likes of us."

"That's none of my affair. I shouldn't be out here. Can you fetch somebody I can talk to? An officer, maybe?"

"Sure, we'll fetch the colonel for you so you and him can have a nice chat. Or maybe you'd rather talk to the general himself," one of the men said. "Why don't you step on over here and hold these rifles for us till we come back."

"You can even put in a little target practice while we're gone," the other soldier laughed. "You can shoot any sonofabitch out there, and tell the sergeant that he said he didn't belong here, neither."

Mel held back what he really wanted to say, and tried one last time. "I'm not a soldier. This is my farm. I just got caught up in this thing."

One of the guards swept the hillside and the surrounding area with his gaze, then turned back to Mel. "You say there was a farm here? I don't see much sign of it."

CHAPTER SEVEN

The prisoners languished in the open field through the endless hot morning as the sun topped the tree line to the east and crawled upward in the sky. Here and there a few more men died, and each time there was a scuffle for his shoes and clothes if anything was worth taking. At another time he might despise the ragged scroungers, but right here, right now, survival was all that mattered. Later they might spend years trying to come to terms with the guilt and shame of what they'd done. But at least they'd be alive to feel the regret.

And who was he to judge anybody? Right now he'd gladly fight any man in the place for a few swallows of water taken off a dead man. But there wasn't any water to fight over.

As morning inched into a sweltering afternoon in the open relentless sunlight, the suffering of the prisoners increased. The scattered rumblings of discontent grew in volume, and groups of men began to collect at the borders of their invisible prison. More guards were added to the ones already on duty, and then more after that. The prisoners pleaded for water, food, and care for their wounded. They taunted the guards openly, and even the shots fired over their heads pushed them back only a few paces.

Mel stayed back away from the ruckus. Nothing could come of this rioting, he thought, except more blood spilled for no gain. But desperate men did desperate things. These were men just one day past being soldiers themselves, ready to fight and die for one cause or another. They hadn't yet been stomped and worn down into dull submission, not like the convicts in the chain gang the county brought through here every year or so to drag and level the post road.

Maybe they had decided it would be better to die right here than away off in whatever prison their enemies sent them to. And maybe they were right. But it was different for Mel. A drink of water wasn't worth dying for. At least not yet.

Some of the captive officers managed to gain control of the situation, possibly stopping a pointless slaughter. Using the powers of command they'd lost a day before, they herded the sullen prisoners back toward the center of the field, then approached the guards to talk. After about ten minutes of negotiation, a deal seemed to be struck.

Before long, two heavily guarded wagons drove into the edge of the prisoner area. From the first wagon buckets of water were filled from large oak barrels and passed down to the prisoners. At the second wagon, each prisoner was given a hunk of dried bread and a dollop of cornmeal mush in a tin cup. It was poor fare and not enough to fill a man's belly, but no one turned it down. There were tiny dark chunks in the grits that Mel thought could be meat, but was more likely bugs. Daddy had told him that eating insects wouldn't hurt a body, and that a man could even live on them unless it was something nasty like spiders or cockroaches, but it was the idea of the thing. Still he ate it, dark bits and all, and scoured the bottom of the cup with his finger to lick off the last dabble.

The empty barrels were carried down to the creek and refilled, then brought back and put on the ground at the edge of the prisoner area so everyone could get what they needed. Now, unexpectedly, there was an abundance of the stuff that the prisoners had nearly been willing to die for an hour before. It didn't make a whit of sense to Mel, but he was glad to quench his thirst nonetheless.

Later he used some of the water to clean the dried blood and dirt from his face. A stranger offered to help, and produced a needle and thread to close the two-inch gash on his cheek. Mel could hardly see out of the eye on that side, and the man who had helped him said he looked like he had a hog jowl stuck to the side of his head.

Those were hardly encouraging words, but the gash was closed and the eye worked at least a little, so he knew he was better off than some of the others. Hardly a man there was unscathed, and some had festering, painful, fly-covered wounds that did not bode well for them. Hour by hour, the line of bodies waiting for burial grew longer.

Mel wandered the area of confinement, looking for any possibility of escape, but it seemed useless. There was too much open ground on all sides, and too many armed men ready to cut down any reckless soul who made a run for it.

He remembered following old Doc over this very ground not so long ago, a man alone turning the middles, passing the long hours thinking about a girl. It seemed now like a snippet out of somebody else's life.

Plowing was work for the body, not the mind. It left countless hours for a man's thoughts to wander in any direction he chose, and sometimes they explored down unexpected pathways he'd never picked at all. Other times his thoughts were entirely predictable, especially for a young man whose sap was rising, with most of his best years still ahead.

There were times when it took no more than a whiff of honeysuckle on the wind, or a cloud shaped a particular way, or the trickle of the brook that sounded almost like laughter, to bring women to mind. And once there, they settled in and stayed for a while.

Before Rochelle Adderly, he had let his mind stray with a

number of local belles. There was the mayor's daughter down in Palestine, a spirited young redhead whose irresistible smile and quick, challenging laughter easily compensated for her smugness and saucy tongue. There was the gypsy woman, seen only once but never forgotten, who danced a harlot's dance with her flailing skirts, and promised many wicked pleasures with a single glance of her ebony eyes. There had been others as well.

But Rochelle, who was real and available, had somehow managed to crowd all the others out of Mel's thoughts, plans, and imaginings. It was easy to recall words that had actually been said, and things that had really happened. Some of the things he remembered would have set a stiff-necked old goose like her father, Ezekiel Adderly, reaching for his twelve-gauge. Mel had last seen Rochelle over a month ago at a dance at the schoolhouse over at Bright's Crossing, and what happened that night sealed the deal for him.

He made no claim to understand women. But he had received a revelation that night, with a clumsy male sense of wonder, that there was no real telling what a young woman would do when the moon was up, and she was hot and close in a man's arms, too far from the watchful eyes of parents to think about consequences. On a Saturday night like that, all the Sunday morning rules and prohibitions could dissolve away like sugar in water.

That's what he had been remembering last week, the day before this lot arrived, while he turned the middles on this very same plot of ground—hot, damp kisses tasting of apple punch and corn liquor, forbidden fumbling explorations, gasps and pants and sighs, and finally, tears of guilt and wonder.

That night they hadn't talked about marriage, or even love. But what else was there for them after what they did? It all seemed clear to Mel during the long ride home after the dance.

But in the solitary days that followed, all kinds of doubts and hesitations flooded his mind. What if Ezekiel Adderly wouldn't give his daughter up to an unchurched heathen like Mel? Or worse, what would Ezekiel do if he found out what Mel and his daughter had been up to in that soft patch of fescue out behind the schoolhouse stable?

And what kind of wife would Rochelle make? Daddy had cautioned him more than once that some women who were sweet as molasses pie during the courtship could turn about on a thimble once the knot was tied. If you wanted to know the future of a woman, Daddy cautioned, look at her mother.

Rochelle's mother was drab as dirt, a relentless nag even with Ezekiel himself, seeming to judge the whole world around her with sour, outspoken disapproval.

Would Rochelle end up being that way over time? Would she make him give up the jug, pester him over every little clod tracked inside, throw up to him what other people had, or hound him to meeting every Sunday? Surely not, Mel decided. Could the girl who had given him what she had given him that night at Bright's Crossing change so much? If he and Rochelle married for love, things would be different for them, wouldn't they? Daddy had warned him once that a man alone had too much time to worry and gnaw over whatever was top of his mind. "It's like spitting in the milk, son," he'd said. "It don't ruin the milk, but it makes it harder to swallow."

With food in his belly and his thirst quenched, other bodily needs began to have their turn. He found a patch of open ground and lay down on the bare dirt, then drifted off to sleep wondering if anything this bad had happened over yonder at the Adderly place. After all he'd seen here, he couldn't convince himself that the distant rumbles off to the west a few nights ago were really a thunderstorm blowing through.

When he woke there was a man sitting on the ground beside him, his knees pulled up, idly watching the scattered throng of prisoners. The sun had dipped down into the fringes of the tree line to the west, bringing some relief from the blistering sun. The spring rains were past and the summer heat was coming early this year. Planting time would probably be too far past to put even a late corn crop in the ground after this lot had gone.

The man beside Mel was as filthy and ragged as all the rest. Much of his head was wrapped in loose dirty bandages, leaving only one eye, his nose, mouth, and jaw exposed. His lips and chin were red as raw meat, and it was obvious that he'd been burned. Mel watched him for a moment, wondering why he was there.

"You don't recognize me, do you?" the man said. His voice was a harsh whisper, and his mouth twisted into what might have been a smile.

"I guess not," Mel said.

"I'm Elliott," the man said. "Major Elliott."

"Yeah, sure, I know you now. Glad you made it this far," Mel said.

"I've been wondering what happened to you after we sent you down into the woods yesterday morning."

"That didn't end well," Mel said. He didn't add that the only good part of the whole escapade was having the chance to settle his sights between that lieutenant's shoulder blades. "I looked around for you later, but things were already going to hell by then."

"When it was nearly too late already, the colonel sent me down here to the cornfield to help rally the line. But after they flanked us I could see that there wasn't any use. Finally I ran away like almost everybody else did."

"So how'd you get hurt? It looks like burns."

"My rifle barrel was plugged with dirt and I tried to fire it. The charge blew back in my face. It hurts like the devil, but it's not as bad as it looks. I was blinded for a while, and that's how they captured me," Elliott said. Then he added, "That's a nasty whack you got on the side of your head too."

"Yep, a fellow proved to me that my skull's not as hard as a rifle stock," Mel said.

"And now they think you're one of us," Elliott said solemnly.

"Seems so."

Mel found out from Elliott about the plans for this group of prisoners. "They told our officers they plan to move us to their rear so there's less chance for us to get back into the fight," the major explained. "But they can't spare the men right now. They're preparing for a counterattack from General Willard's main force, and they just might get one."

"What happens to this bunch if that happens?" Mel asked.

"God only knows. They sure won't feel easy about having this many men at their backs while they're facing an attack in front."

"So maybe they'll shoot the lot of you and be done with it. Or shoot us, I s'pose."

"I can't see Paul Calverton ordering anything as dishonorable as that. He's one of the best generals they have in this theater, and I'd gamble he has something a little less drastic worked out."

"You talk like you know the man," Mel said.

"We were in the same graduating class at Ole Miss. I've visited his home in Saint Louis any number of times when I was there on business. He's a fine man, and I count him a friend."

"But here the two of you are slinging bullets at each other. Until yesterday, at least."

Elliott shook his head, and the half smile briefly twisted his mouth again. "War's a strange business."

Mel learned that Elliott would soon lead one of the burial details, and he asked to go along. Anything beat sitting on the bare ground out here in the cornfield, and who knew what opportunity might offer itself.

Soon, with guards in tow, the detail of prisoners began loading the bodies of their less lucky comrades into the bed of a wagon, then drove down to the current spot being used as a burying ground. A long shallow trench had been dug in Mel's south pasture, and over half of it was already filled with bodies and covered over.

The men worked listlessly in the fading evening light, but the guards didn't seem to mind. As the daylight failed, one guard lit a lamp and hung it on a pole attached to the back of the wagon so the work could continue.

Mel and Elliott tugged a body to the rear of the wagon, then lifted it off and carried it to the trench. Both men stepped down into the shallow trench to situate the corpse into the position it would remain in for eternity. The man they were laying to rest looked to be in his thirties, a simple laborer judging by his calloused hands and worn work boots. His body was violated in so many places that Mel couldn't even guess how he might have died. This much damage must have been caused by one of those exploding cannonballs, which was an infernal invention if ever mankind created one. But there was also a hole in his throat below his neck that looked like a bullet hole, and could have been what took him.

But it didn't really matter in the end. Dead was dead whether chunks of you were scattered around somebody's cornfield, or you breathed your last breath in a soft feather bed. And your soul still moved on to where it belonged, which could be a pure blessing from the Lord, or terrible beyond a man's imagining.

"It's worse when you know them," Elliott said.

"You knew this man?" Mel asked.

"Kyle Jones from Elaine. His wife was dead, but he had children, I believe. Hard drinker when he could lay his hands on something. But likeable."

"Why do you do this, Major? You're hurt yourself and in charge. You could order somebody else to bury these men."

"I need to see the bodies so I can remember as many as possible. If I make it through myself, I'd like to let some of the families know where and how it happened. In my version they'll all be heroes, stopping an enemy charge, saving the colors, and suchlike."

"Instead of throwing their rifles down and running like jackrabbits?"

"My reports won't have any stories like that," Elliott said quietly.

When Kyle Jones was situated on his back close beside a comrade Elliott identified as Felix Hamm, arms folded, eyes closed, wounds now unimportant, the major sat down on the edge of the trench. Mel sat beside him, figuring it must be okay because nobody ordered them to get back to work.

"I've given this some thought, Mr. Carroll," the major said, "and I think it's time to bury you too."

The comment puzzled Mel. "I'm beat up and bloodied," he said, "but I don't think I'm ready for that quite yet."

"Maybe I can convince you otherwise."

"Then have a run at it," Mel offered.

"Tomorrow, or at least sometime soon," Elliott said, "they'll march us out of here. As soon as they can get us to a railhead, they'll herd us into cattle cars and take us north to a camp, who knows where, to sit out the war. From what I've heard, it probably won't be a very pleasant place to spend the next few months . . . or years."

"I couldn't tolerate that," Mel said. "I'd die fighting here on my own place before I let them do that to me."

"That's why you're better off buried."

Mel began to understand the logic of it. "How long you figure

I could breathe down there before I ran out of air?" he asked.

"I don't know that," Elliott admitted. "But I have heard of men buried alive and making it out okay. You could keep a little space open around your face, and the dirt's dry and loose. We wouldn't tamp it down around your head."

Mel looked down at the freshly laid out Kyle Jones and estimated that when the job was finished, he'd have no more than sixteen or eighteen inches of dirt on top of him.

"There's one more thing, though," Elliott said. "The guards will probably come along after and shove their bayonets into the dirt. We'll have to put you under another body so you won't get stuck."

"Well, hell," Mel said. He looked down at Jones again and imagined himself buried not beside him, but under him. He didn't allow his mind to dwell on what that might feel like, two feet underground with a dead man on top of him, fighting for every breath. It seemed like a man might lose all his sense in a mess like that. But maybe not.

Over in the back of the wagon the guards had become more interested in a wine bottle and a pair of dice than they were in the men they were charged with guarding.

"There's no better time than now," Elliott said, pointing down into the trench. As he stood up and started back to the wagon for another body, Mel dropped down onto his knees beside Jones. He scooped extra dirt away from the spot where he would be buried, and dug out an even deeper hole below where his head would be. He laid facedown in the trench and pulled his shirt up over his head, then held it in place with one arm hooked over the top of his head. He kept his other arm bent and tight at his side, palm down, ready to push up with all the strength he could muster once the time came.

"Lay him in gently, Hasty," Elliott whispered urgently to the man who helped bring the next body over. Mel felt the weight placed carefully, head to foot, on top of him. Then Elliott knelt to arrange the dead man's body, as he had with Jones. He tilted his head forward and said quietly, "I pray God lays himself down here beside you, Mr. Carroll."

Mel lay still while the final few bodies were brought over and placed in the grisly row of corpses. Then the dirt began to fall. Mel controlled an almost overwhelming urge to wrestle himself free as the first shovelful of dirt landed on the back of his head, but he clenched his jaw and let it happen.

In the next few minutes he was submerged into a new existence where light, sound and movement were all denied him. The air in the hole beneath his face slowly became stale and unsatisfying. The weight of the body and dirt on top of him was oppressive. An itch in the middle of his back quickly became maddening.

Long minutes passed, and Mel concentrated on taking slow, shallow breaths, which seemed to suffice. He began to relax, almost as if he was going to sleep, and he wondered if there was any danger in that. He imagined himself drifting into a stupor for want of breathable air, dying unresisting.

Then unexpected panic gripped him without warning. Cold, slimy sweat oozed from his skin, and every muscle in his body seemed to tingle and ache. He sucked in panting draughts of useless air. He fought the urge to shove his body upward out of this living grave and into the cool, clean night air above. It was too soon. Too soon. Somehow he coaxed himself into believing that he could at least bear another minute of this hell, and then another minute, and another . . .

His breathing started to slow again, and the panic began to bleed out of him.

Fresh clean air waited for him up there, but so did men with rifles and bayonets, and that first sweet breath might also be his last. He breathed even shallower, willing his body to relax, his heart to slow, his nerves to calm.

He could bear this just a minute longer.

Mel felt an added pressure on top of his legs and knew someone had stepped on his grave. The body on top of him pressed down harder for an instant, then wiggled eerily. That would be the bayonet going in, twisting for the release, then withdrawing. Elliott was right. The guards were no fools, but they hadn't thought of everything. Nor had they counted heads, apparently.

A moment later the body to his side, Felix Hamm, jarred, shook, then stilled.

Mel thought about his breathing—slower, shallower—and willed his body and mind to hold on. Some traces of air must be reaching him somehow or he would be dead already. But it wasn't enough, not nearly enough. Time passed, seconds or minutes, who knew, in absolute darkness, absolute silence, absolute stillness. He could feel his own heart trying harder and harder to keep him alive. Pinpricks of light flashed behind his eyelids. His brain filled with cobwebs, and he couldn't put any clear thoughts together.

When he felt the slight trembling he thought it was his own body, giving up perhaps. Then he knew it wasn't him, but the ground under him. The wagon was leaving, rumbling and bumping over the uneven pasture. He might not be able to see or hear anything, but feeling this, and knowing what it was, was like a gift from the Almighty. He imagined the wagon's progress. Thirty feet away, now forty, now fifty, the cemetery already out of sight in the darkness.

Mel tried to push up with his numb right arm, but it, like the rest of him, was immobilized by the weight of the body and the dirt on top of him. He tried again, pushing desperately, and nearly blacked out as his air-starved muscles struggled to follow his commands. The only real movement he could manage was a little side-to-side wiggle of his head and shoulders, so he kept doing that, knowing that any movement was better than none. The body on top of him began to shift, and he encouraged it with more side-to-side wiggles.

Eventually the body began to slide off of him, and finally they lay side by side, head to foot, in the grave. Someone had stolen the man's boots, and his dirty rotting feet smelled unimaginable.

Once free of the dead weight of the corpse, Mel quickly scratched and clawed his way to the surface, sucking in great gulps of clean, cool air. He was dizzy with the great joy and relief of it. At that moment the starlit sky seemed to be the most beautiful vision of his life. Even the sights and sounds of the occupying army were welcome to his senses after the horrifying void of silence and darkness underground.

This army was bigger than the one that had first taken over his farm. Their tents and camps and wagons had spilled over into the open pasture beyond where the graveyard was located. But none were close. The smell from the shallow graves would soon thicken the air with the rancid odor of decaying flesh, and what man could rest easy if he slept too near so many departed souls?

The smell of their food and the blaze of their fires was inviting, but he knew he couldn't walk up and ask for a bowl of stew like he had before. Different army, different dangers.

The foot of the man Mel was buried under was sticking up out of the grave. Mel shoved it back down into the loose dirt, then tried to smooth the top of the grave as best he could. He felt an odd sort of bond with the man now. They had shared a grave, after all, and the fellow had taken a bayonet stab that could easily have made Mel a permanent resident.

Clearly he had to make his way beyond the army's perimeter and far away before sunrise. Rose Creek seemed his best chance for that. The little creek wound and ambled west to east across the farm, forming a natural division between cropland and pasture and providing a convenient source of water for his cattle. Its banks were steep and brushy in most places, except for the cuts Mel and his father had made to allow the cattle access to the water. One of those cuts also served as a crossing for their farm road.

Mel considered crawling the fifty-yard stretch to the creek for caution's sake, but he wasn't sure his starved, battered body was up to it. Instead, he stood up and walked the distance in the clear moonlight, like a man should be able to do on his own land, he thought. He made it without challenge. All eyes in the camp were looking outward tonight, it seemed, or staring into dying fires and wondering what tomorrow had in store.

When he reached the creek he stripped naked and washed both himself and his clothes. He washed his head wound, then examined it carefully with his fingers. It was swollen, painful to the touch, and slightly feverish. But he was beginning to see better out of the eye on that side, which he took to be a positive sign.

Redressing, he started cautiously downstream, using stealth and alertness honed fine by a lifetime of tracking and hunting. At one point he discovered a bloated corpse facedown in the creek that had been missed by the burial details. Judging by the smell, mother earth's process of drawing the man to her bosom was well under way. There were no weapons anywhere about, but Mel's reluctant search of the dead man did yield a sheath knife with a heavy ten-inch blade, and a flint and steel for fire starting. Both would be useful in the wilderness where he planned to go.

Near the edge of the property where the pickets were stationed, he went down on his belly and crawled along the gravel bed of the creek, keeping only his head above the water's rippling surface. The pickets atop the steep bank, no more than twenty feet from him, continued their quiet grumblings about army life and lousy chow, unaware of his passing.

It was a fine uplifting feeling to be clear of the camp, but the irony of the situation was not lost on him. Who knew it would take such a difficult, desperate effort to escape from his own land and from the captivity of an army mustered from his own state? It was harder day by day to figure out who to hate and who to be grateful to.

An enormous sense of relief settled over Mel as he entered the familiar woods east of his farm. Everything he needed to survive was in these woods, and a thousand men would have the devil of a time flushing him out if he didn't want to be found. But as it was, nobody even knew he was gone except the one real friend he had made in all this madness and confusion, Major Elliot—a man he was not likely to ever encounter again here on this earth.

★ ★ ★ ★ ★

Part Two
The Adderly Farm Rescue

★ ★ ★ ★ ★

CHAPTER EIGHT

Mel woke with a start to the sound of rustling and grunting at the edge of the cane thicket. He knew it was probably the hog that had taken up residence here, voicing his complaints about an uninvited squatter. He cautiously drew the sheath knife and stood up facing the commotion.

"Git, hog!" he called out, loud and gruff, kicking the nearby cane stalks and making as much commotion as he could. If it was one of his own pigs, that would be enough. And if it was one of the wild, mean razorbacks that roamed all through these mountains, at least he could make a fight of it with the knife. "Git, hog. Git on out of here!" Eventually the hog wandered away, grunting and snorting its offense at the injustice.

Mel settled back on the ground, lying flat on his back with his head resting on a hump of sod, enjoying the feel of the cool morning breeze, listening to the soft rustle of the cane tops, watching the feathery clouds floating past against the bright blue sky.

In spite of everything, it felt good to be alive on God's green earth. Being buried alive and shoving the dead aside to rise again would do that for a man. So for a while he just lay there letting his senses take charge, not worrying about anything that had already happened, or what was ahead.

He was staggering with fatigue when he reached this spot last night. The moon was down before he made it here, but these were home woods and he trusted his instincts to guide him to the one place where he knew he would feel hidden and secure. From the moment he lay his head down on the soft carpet of leaves and moss in the cane thicket, to the instant when the grumbling hog woke him, he hadn't moved a muscle or stirred awake for an instant. He wasn't sure he had even dreamed.

Mel felt rested, at ease in his mind about his own safety, at least for now. But he was as hungry as a spring cub, and his smarting, throbbing wounds reminded him of the abuse his body had taken over the past few days.

When he sat up again, he noticed the squirrel for the first time. It lay near his feet, its head half gone, skull open and empty. It was a familiar sight, one he had found countless times lying on the back step of the cabin or on the ground nearby. Looking around in the cane thicket, he spotted the shaggy matted bundle of gray fur hunkered down on its haunches a dozen feet away.

"Hello, Smokie," Mel said with a smile. "Glad to see you made it through all this mess."

Smokie had been his mother's pet cat, roaming in and out of the cabin at will, spending the evenings in her lap as she mended clothes, shelled beans, or read by the fire, earning his found by keeping the rodent population down. But when Mother passed, Smokie never had taken to Mel or his father in the same way. Over time he lapsed into a feral life, lurking around the barn and outbuildings but shunning the cabin, staying near but never close, bedding who knew where, and feeding himself in his own mysterious ways.

The one habit he maintained even after the passing of his mistress was his almost daily contributions of meat for the household. The fresh kills varied. One morning it might be a rat or chipmunk, the next a squirrel or rabbit or bird. Mel never could figure out why he did it, and of course the gifts were never eaten. But Smokie didn't seem to notice.

This morning, though, down in the cane thicket, everything was different, and he had the distinct feeling that the old ragged gray cat was looking out for him, sharing the night's kill so he wouldn't go hungry. And for the first time in his recollection, he was glad to see the mangy old cat, and the fresh meat was actually welcome.

"Much obliged for breakfast, old feller," Mel said, lifting the squirrel and saluting Smokie with it. He deftly skinned and gutted it, cut off the head, wrapped it in a bundle of leaves, and stuck it in his pocket for later when he had the chance to safely build a fire. When Mel looked up after a few minutes, Smokie had disappeared, his mission completed.

Mel worked his way out of the dense cane thicket, moving stealthily. He was still within half a mile of his farm, and if its occupiers had any sense, they would have patrols out in the woods. But Mel was confident that he would hear them before they heard him, and here on his home ground, none of them would see him unless he chose to be seen.

At the creek flowing alongside Dogleg Trail, he stripped naked and gave his clothes and body another good scrubbing. The bullet nick on his shoulder was healing, but the gash the rifle butt had made on the side of his head was starting to fester. He scrubbed off the bloody scab with a handful of moss, then let the wound bleed and cleanse itself. The creek ran pink with his blood for a while until he packed a hunk of sphagnum moss over the wound and tied it in place with a strip torn from his shirt.

It wasn't as good as cleaning a wound with a splash of corn liquor, or dealing with the smart of it with a long hard pull on the jug, but it would serve for now.

Filling his hollow, complaining belly came next. He had the squirrel for a main course, and for someone who knew what he was about, the woods were filled with many other edibles. In the creek there were crawdads that skittered backward under rocks at his approach, and minnows in the shallow pools that could be netted with a shirt or caught by hand. There were watercress and other edible plants in the pools. Mushrooms grew on the forest floor and the rotting trunks of trees, some delicious and some deadly. Even the beetles, grubs, worms and snails that flourished under rocks and fallen trees were edible and said to be nourishing. But Mel gagged at the thought of it, and figured he'd have to be nearer to starving than he was now before he'd choke down any bugs.

He risked a small fire in a sheltered gully along the creek, using dry kindling that hardly smoked. While strips of squirrel and little slivers of meat from the crawdad tails cooked on a hot rock, he ate the rest of his foraged meal raw, even the minnows, whose heads he pinched off before swallowing them.

While he ate he thought about what came next. Returning to his own farm was no longer possible, so only one choice seemed left for him. He would head over to the Adderly farm and see how Rochelle and her family had fared through all of this. Getting there would be hard, though, as the major had warned. Both armies seemed bent on controlling the roads, and they probably wouldn't be interested in allowing a lone man pass, no matter what errand he claimed to be on.

The valley and meadows that threaded through the steep wooded hillsides were another possibility. But there was no guarantee that he wouldn't find some of them full-up with fighting men, too. The army that had fought their way up the length of White Tail Valley must have traveled overland for many miles, and there were no roads out where they came from.

A thought occurred to Mel as he stuck the last dry, tough strips of squirrel meat into his back pocket and kicked the embers of his fire into the creek. He still had one unlikely ally nearby. He started carefully up Dogleg Trail, pausing often to look around, listen, and test the wind. It was an enormous risk moving toward his farm rather than away, but it had to be done.

At the crest of the hill where he had put the Arkansas lieutenant down with a sweet, clean shot in the back, he stopped and inspected the brush and weeds around him. Now, three days after, there wasn't much left in the vicinity that resembled a human body. The forest creatures had been working hard at their trade, some of them possibly Mel's own hogs. The scattered tracks in the dirt included cloven hoofprints, as well as the larger, five-padded prints of wolves and wild dogs, and the splayed, taloned prints of buzzards. He imagined that there had probably been some lively disagreements about who ate first, and who got what.

Random bones and mangled scraps of clothing were scattered up and down the trail and in the surrounding brush. Scouting about, he found one boot, a fine expensive one in fairly good shape, but clearly too small for him. The lieutenant's skull was a mangled, grisly find, and he gave it wide berth. It occurred to Mel that this man's people down in the Arkansas Delta would never know what became of him. Over time they'd probably make a hero out of him, and maybe attribute preposterous heroic deeds to him. Even if they somehow miraculously heard the truth about him—that he had thrown away the lives of his men with bad leadership during a fool's mission, and was shot in the back by a stranger because he was such a loudmouthed little jaybird—they would never accept it. But Mel figured they had a right to believe what they wanted of him if it gave them comfort.

Soon Mel found what he was searching for, the lieutenant's rifle, sidearm, and ammunition. The pistol belt and holster were chewed a bit, but still usable, and a feeling of relief came over him as he strapped them on. He was a different man, no longer a defenseless creature hiding in the weeds like a weasel, as soon

121

as he was armed again. Both the rifle and pistol would need cleaning and fresh charges, but already they felt like trusted comrades in his hands.

The overland route he chose to the Adderly Farm would lead him in a loop around the north end of White Tail Valley. During the fight for his farm, this would have been the rear area for the attacking men in blue. Although this end of the valley was deserted now, there was plenty of evidence that thousands of men had passed this way. All the cast-off waste and flotsam of an army moving dynamically with the tides of battle were there. And in this case, the "waste" included rows and rows of graves for the men who had not, and never would, move on with their comrades to the next battle.

Mel was surprised by his own reaction to the hundreds of graves, so fresh that the wind still stirred up dust as it blew over the dry untamped dirt. Chills washed over him, as when spirits are passing by, and he didn't let his eyes or thoughts linger long on this land of the dead. His own experience as a buried man himself was still too fresh a horror.

Before moving on, he did manage to salvage a few things that might come in handy—a cast-off rucksack, a hatchet, a pair of socks, a few yards of decent hemp rope, and a wine bottle that would serve nicely for water.

White Tail Valley curved west on its northern end, and Mel could have followed it for miles in the direction he wanted to go. But he was ill at ease out in the open for too long, even though he had not seen another living person since waking that morning. So he stuck to the edge of the woods as much as possible, as was his habit while hunting. With elk, deer, bear or man, the idea was to spot them before they spotted you. That gave you the choice of what happened next.

His progress was steady, although he could feel the toll that several days of hard living, poor food, and physical abuse had taken. Moving through the forest with his long, farm-boy strides, he refused to let his thoughts dwell on the destroyed home and razed farm he left behind, or the devastation and suffering he might find ahead.

Instead he turned his thoughts to Rochelle. When it came right down to it, he knew that the hard and dangerous trip he had ahead of him was really all about her. Otherwise, why wouldn't he have set his mind to check on Ike and Martha Butternut, who lived a few miles southwest of his farm, or Jared Hardt, who ran the sawmill ten miles west along the post road? There were other neighbors hereabouts, none close, but all as likely to be in danger as the Adderlys while this uninvited war tore, stomped, destroyed and slaughtered its way across the countryside.

In his thoughts he pictured Rochelle as he had last seen her, tan, slender and pretty, shy as a sparrow, but mostly a ripe, full-grown woman already. Countless times following old Doc across the fresh-turned furrows of his fields, or laying alone at night in his pitch-dark cabin, he had brought to mind the memory of that backwoods community dance, and the incredible turmoil of love and need, guilt and wonder, that had washed over them on that grassy hillside out back of the one-room log schoolhouse. Once they had started down that path, neither one of them could have stopped it.

He had lived in close quarters with his parents long enough to know that marriage wasn't always a smooth downhill ride. There were squabbles, deprivation, hard times and hard work aplenty for people who lived their isolated lives far out in the hills like this. But knowing that marriage would also include plenty more of what he had experienced that night with Rochelle, warm and hungry in his arms, tipped the scale heavy to the good side.

A storm blew through in early afternoon, sweeping in fast

and angry. The trees whipped and lashed, and for a short time the sheets of windblown rain grayed the landscape and obliterated anything more than a few yards away.

Mel hunkered down against the trunk of a huge spreading cedar, not getting quite as soaked as he might have out in the open. It wasn't the kind of rain that farmers prayed for, falling fast and heavy, and mostly running off instead of soaking in like a soft, steady, all-day rain. But any kind of rain was better than no rain, and he imagined how welcome this downpour would have been to his fledgling rows of corn. Now there was no corn to worry about.

After the storm moved past, racing hard and determined to the northeast, Mel emerged from his shelter into a dripping, suddenly sunlit world, as fresh and clean as the day the Lord made it. He wrung his shirt nearly dry, then sat on a log to wipe his guns down and check the loads. Daddy had shared grisly stories about what sometimes happened to men with damp powder in an Indian fight, and the lesson had stuck.

At the edge of the woods where the trees began to thin, a six-point buck stepped out of a blackberry thicket and paused to look around for threats. He was a fine animal, healthy and proud, his sleek brown hide still dripping rainwater. He hadn't yet detected Mel, who stood unmoving beside the trunk of an oak tree.

Mel knew that when the buck looked away he could raise his rifle and take the shot. But he wouldn't. It would be an insult to such a fine animal to end its life and then leave most of its meat as carrion. He was hungry, but he could wait until other food presented itself. A man who knew what he was about could always find something to fill his empty belly in woods like these.

In a minute the buck seemed to sense Mel's presence, possibly catching his scent on the breeze. Its gaze fixed in his direction, seeking any sign of movement that would confirm danger.

And then it was gone, whirling and leaping away so abruptly that it actually startled Mel.

The buck burst into the open valley, heading toward the denser woods on the other side, covering ground with the long healthy bounds that never failed to make Mel's heart pound with excitement. But he didn't make it. The bullet struck him broadside, punching him sideways in mid-leap and rolling him clumsily in the knee-high grass. The crack of the rifle shot sounded an instant later, echoing for a moment down the valley before dying away. Mel didn't know who or where the shooter was, but he admired the marksmanship. Dropping a grown buck like that running full-out over open ground was no common feat.

The buck was thrashing on the ground and Mel figured he still had some run left in him. The stamina and will of even a severely wounded deer was astounding. More than once he had spent hours following the blood trail of a wounded deer that, by the rules of nature, should have fallen dead where it was shot.

This buck fully intended to die someplace else on his own terms, but as he struggled to his feet and started forward again, a second shot, skillfully placed to the front of his chest, dropped him dead.

He heard the sound of horses approaching down the valley from the west. For better cover, Mel dropped a few yards back into the forest. There were about thirty riders in the group, gaunt, dusty, hard-featured men mounted on the kind of sturdy, blooded horseflesh that Mel could scarcely imagine ever owning. There wasn't much about them that gave Mel any clues about which army they were with. But it really didn't matter. Both sides were equally dangerous to him now.

When they reached the fallen buck, one of the riders who seemed to be in charge gave an order, and most of the horsemen dismounted. A few stayed in the saddle, scattering out in all directions around the main band. That was their version of sentries, Mel supposed. A couple of the outriders rode closer to where he was. He knew the sensible thing would be to get out of there, but he was well concealed, and curiosity kept him from leaving just yet.

The men who dismounted by the deer began to fill their pipes, roll smokes, drink from their canteens, and gnaw bits of food they took from their saddlebags. A couple of them fell to work cleaning and quartering the deer, and tying the pieces on some of the horses. They'd have roast venison for supper tonight, and most of them looked like they needed it.

The outriders closest to Mel patrolled the edge of the woods restlessly, obviously on guard for any sign that their party might be at risk of attack. Every time they came near him, he hunkered down until he heard the hoofbeats of their horses move on by.

The rattle of gunfire flared up unexpectedly, then died away, somewhere down the long valley to the east. It was no more than a score of shots, but enough to signal trouble. The horsemen near where the buck had fallen leaped into their saddles and readied their weapons. Clearly they were used to this kind of thing, because there was no panic or confusion. But instead of riding off, they pranced their horses around restlessly, waiting as the outriders rejoined the main group. Of the three who rode off down the valley, only two came back. The third riderless horse trotted along behind.

The two men made their report to their leader, pointing repeatedly to the east, then he conferred with some of the others. They seemed uncertain what to do, and Mel figured it could be because they didn't know how many opponents they were up against. When a decision was made, two men separated themselves from the rest and rode hard to the west. The rest rode east, toward where the shots were fired, screaming their battle cries.

It didn't take them long to pass out of Mel's line of sight. He risked moving to the edge of the woods and even stepped out into the open for a better look. But they were gone, and for a few moments tranquility seemed to have returned.

That didn't last long. When the shooting started he was tempted to hurry in that direction to see if he could watch the fight. He was curious how men fought from horseback, thinking that if he ever did get dragged into this mess, that would suit him better than being afoot.

But he didn't have to move forward to the fight, because the fight began to roll back toward him. When the band of mounted men came back into view, they were short a few men and horses. Clearly they had run into more fight down there than they knew what to do with. They rode flat-out hunched forward over the necks of their mounts, not looking back, not shooting, intent only on escape.

Seconds later Mel heard, then saw, the reason for their flight. Two or three hundred yards behind them dozens, perhaps hundreds, of mounted men were racing up the valley after them.

On some signal from their leader, the fleeing men began to scatter, each man seeming to choose his own route either up the valley or into the bordering forest. One of them cut his horse sharply left and began streaking toward where Mel stood. Only then did Mel realize that, like a dolt, he was still standing out in the open. By the time he leaped back into the edge of the woods, the man had drawn a pistol and was firing wildly in his direction. But nothing connected, and within seconds the gun was empty.

Mel figured he still had a fight on his hands, and ran like a rabbit deeper into the woods. When the sound of the horse's hooves sounded ready to crawl up his backbone, he threw himself off to the side, hitting the ground hard and rolling in the damp leaves and humus of the forest floor.

The rider cursed him desperately as he thundered past, and seemed to fling something dark and heavy in Mel's direction. In an instant he had disappeared into the woods ahead, leaving behind only the vague familiar stench of leather, horse sweat, and fear.

Mel started to rise, then changed his mind. Back toward the open valley, a group of pursuing horsemen had broken away from the main band and were hot after the soldier who almost rode Mel down seconds before. Crawling forward, he burrowed into the dense, thorny undergrowth of a blackberry thicket, then lay still until the pursuing horsemen passed.

Intermittent gunfire started popping from several directions, some near, some distant, all confusing. Mel worked his way carefully out of the blackberry thicket, but still didn't get up. This wasn't like the fighting he had seen before when the two sides went at it nose to nose until one side or the other had enough. This fight was broken up and scattered out. How did they even know who to shoot at?

Mel knew he had to leave this dangerous spot, but he had no clear idea which way was best. There seemed to be little pockets of fighting all around him, and with everyone mounted and riding hell-bent this way and that, how could anyone know where it would break out next?

Finally he decided that, with no better choice to make, he'd do what instinct and sound reason told him. He'd head for the deep woods. That meant going due south, the direction the lone rider and his pursuers had taken.

As he started to rise, his hand rested on something firm and moist. Brushing the leaves away, he was surprised to find a haunch of the deer the men in the valley had killed and butchered earlier. That, Mel realized, must have been what came at him when the rider raced by him.

As a hungry man not eager to build another meal of squirrels, crawdads and water plants, Mel took it as a good omen. He'd fill his belly with venison tonight, providing he could find a place secluded enough to build a fire and roast his prize. He stuck the haunch in his pack and gave his guns another going-over before starting out. He wasn't as familiar with these woods as he was with the ones closer to home. But he knew enough not to get lost, and enough to be able to chart a new route to the Adderly farm when an opportunity came along.

Somewhere a couple of miles to the south was Vesper Mountain, a rugged, heavily wooded outbreak of rock that nobody would ever be tempted to climb without an important reason. The country around Vesper Mountain was nearly as forbidding, slashed with deep ravines, jagged stone outcroppings, and dense, nearly impenetrable forest and undergrowth. Local legend had it that a breed of tall hairy ape-men had once lived in there, and that hunters had been known to disappear forever in that vicinity.

Mel had no yearning to confirm or disprove the legends, but he figured if it was as thick and nasty as folks said, it might be a perfectly secluded place for a man to cook a meal and have a few hours of uninterrupted sleep.

He took off south at a trot, pleased to hear the pockets of gunfire fading behind him. The forest floor was level and clear hereabouts, and for the first few minutes he made good time, even with the heavy pack and the weapons he carried.

When he came across the bodies of the horse and rider who had fled in this direction earlier, he sorted out pretty quickly what had happened. The men pursuing him had shot the horse out from under him. The rider was thrown clear as the horse fell, but was killed on the landing. The horse wasn't as lucky. It lay on its side, bleeding heavily but not trying to struggle to its feet. The gurgling rasp of its labored breathing told the story of a lung wound, only its eyes moving as it tracked Mel's cautious approach. Mel dispatched it with a smooth, deep knife stroke across the throat.

There wasn't much at the scene worth taking, but he did remove the belt, holster and revolver from around the dead man's waist and put it in his pack. It was clear enough that while he was in these parts, there was no such thing as having too many firearms.

Gunfire snapped in fits and starts from all directions, some too close for comfort's sake, but most farther away. This whole business was unsettling and confusing. Back at his farm both sides had lined up face-to-face and had at it. Eventually the side with the most men, guns and grit won out. It was bloody and barbaric, but at least a man could get his mind around what was happening.

Out here was different. There were little pockets of fighting all over the place, here now, then somewhere over there next, and then away off yonder someplace. They fought one time on open ground, next in the woods, now in the valleys, and then up the steep hillsides. There weren't any roads back in here, and very few trails except the narrow winding pathways that game followed. There was nothing to defend, no place to capture.

It occurred to Mel that the men on both sides of this scrap probably had little idea where they were or what direction they should go to reach the safety of their own lines. They seem to fight almost for the sport of it, only knowing that if another man had on a shirt and trousers different than their own, that made him fair game.

All of that only made things more difficult for Mel. His clothes weren't the same as anybody else's, so anybody he came across out here was likely to draw a bead and fire away at him for safety's sake.

By sundown he had reached the rugged landscape that marked the fringes of Vesper Mountain. With all the crazy armed men riding around these woods, he was tempted to lose himself in that wild terrain ahead and wait things out. He had meat enough to last at least three days, and was confident that he could find water and shelter in there. The landscape was too broken and perilous for any mounted man.

But he had started this trip with a whole different purpose, and some feeling or instinct told him that if he delayed, it could be too late to be of any help to Rochelle and her family.

As night approached, he settled in to rest and eat in a narrow crevice in the rocks beneath the spreading branches of an ancient oak. He could only be approached from one direction, and the tree would provide some protection if it rained again during the night. He felt reasonably secure there, as secure as anyone could feel in a wilderness landscape peppered with armed, dangerous men.

The night fell far short of being a restful one. Between the random gunfire that still flared up occasionally, and the animals that crept near from time to time, drawn by the smell of his food and his own unfamiliar man scent, he spent most of the nighttime hours only half dozing, startled awake again and again by disruptions far and near.

One particular noise, a few hours before sunup, jangled his nerves like none of the rest. A lifelong woodsman, he prided himself on his ability to identify even the strangest nighttime wilderness sounds. The wild hogs and bears, the various kinds of big cats, the wolves, foxes and coyotes, all had their own set of unique cries, grunts, signals and warnings.

But there was a mournful, almost human, texture to this particular cry that made it different than anything he had ever heard at night in the big woods before. A primal chill made his flesh tingle as it rose almost to a scream of pain, then subsided slowly into something profoundly sorrowful. It was impossible to tell whether the noise came from near or far. The cliffs, caves, winds, and stark rock faces played mysterious games with sounds in these mountains, carrying one on seemingly forever while smothering another almost before it began.

Yet Mel could not shake himself of the eerie feeling that, whatever had made that cry, it knew he was there and possibly meant him harm.

The old front porch and campfire tales of the ghosts and unknown creatures that inhabited Vesper Mountain returned vividly to his mind. It was said that as far back as any white man in these parts could remember, people had been disappearing in the rugged terrain around the mountain. The first settlers had reported unearthly sounds and hair-raising sights, and before them the Indians had passed down similar legends.

It brought Mel little comfort to decide that what he had heard was almost certainly a ghost, or even something worse. His mother had assured him in his childhood that, as frightening as they might be, ghosts were simply sad, mournful spirits that had somehow lost the way during their journey from this life to the next. They were searching, always searching, for they knew not what, and in God's own time they would move on.

But there were also the horrifying tales told by old men who swore they had seen things with their own eyes that were neither man nor ghost nor belonging to the animal kingdom, things that made their hearts stop and their bladders empty in absolute terror.

Off and on the cries continued every few minutes, sometimes seeming far in the distance, and sometimes so close that he raised a cocked revolver in each hand and stared into the pitch darkness until his eyes ached. Finally, he could stand no more of it. Firing wildly into the night, he cut loose with his own chorus of shrieks and howls, defying whatever, or whoever, it was to come on and get it over with.

But no one and nothing came. After that the forest fell deathly silent, as was usual for the predawn hours, and Mel fell into a deep, undisturbed sleep.

CHAPTER NINE

The rain started soon after dawn. Mel crawled stiff-legged and hungry out of the split in the stone, knowing how suddenly such places could fill with surging runoff. Now in the daylight, the terrors of the moonless night seemed far away, as if it had happened to someone else. His mind sought ordinary explanations for the extraordinary things he had heard, even the mournful human-sounding wails and moans. Two tree branches rubbing in the wind, perhaps. Or the death throes of some woodland creature, or even a human being.

He resolved that he might never know for sure unless he spent another night here on a moonless night, which didn't seem likely. But it would make one heck of a yarn anyway.

He struck a course as straight west as the broken terrain would allow, and after the first hour of steady walking, it occurred to him that he had not heard a single gunshot since starting out. Maybe all the scattered bands of fighting men had moved on as unexplainably as they had appeared. Even better, maybe both armies had pulled out of the area. After all, what was there to fight over way out here in these steep hills, dense woods, towering cliffs, and winding valleys? This area was so remote that there were no roads to it, and nobody had even thought about settling out here.

That gave him hope that he could complete his trip to the Adderly farm without further risk and delay. And maybe he would find them all safe. Maybe the war had moved right on past them without stopping to ruin everything, as it had at his place.

A sudden crazy idea came to Mel, and, as he turned the thing over and over in his mind, looking at it from all sides, it began take a hold on him. What would happen if, when he first reached the Adderly place, and the instant he laid eyes on Rochelle, he came right out and declared his intentions to her and her parents? It was the honorable thing to do, and maybe they might even let him stay on and help work their fields until the fall crops were in and he and Rochelle were properly wed. There wasn't much to return to at his place, and he could spend the winter building a new cabin for himself and his bride. He might even give some thought to a frame house with sawed plank walls if he could somehow come up with the money for the lumber.

That gave him plenty to think about over the next couple of hours as his long legs moved him closer to his destination. Old Ezekiel Adderly might be a trial to get along with day in and out over the next summer and fall, but at least he was a man of the cloth. The way Mel saw it, he and Rochelle could tie the knot any time they chose because her daddy could marry them.

The earlier rain slackened to a drizzle and then stopped altogether. By mid morning the sky was clear and the sun was midway up in the sky behind him. He stopped for a time to dry and reload his rifle and the holstered gun at his waist. He cooked a few slices of venison over a damp, smoky fire before starting up again.

He came across the next dead man in a creek-lined draw between two steep, forested hills. The buzzards and crows scattered reluctantly as Mel approached, but settled on the low tree limbs nearby waiting expectantly for him to pass on by. The man's face and hands were a torn bloody mess from their work, but the larger animals hadn't gotten to him yet, so his parts weren't scattered.

Mel retrieved another handgun from the corpse, although the weight of the pack was becoming cumbersome with weaponry. He also took a fine-looking pocket watch that was still ticking, and some odd paper money that might or might not have any value once the armies had taken their fight someplace else.

He felt uneasy at the realization that he was becoming almost comfortable with the notion of robbing the dead. Back at the farm he had scorned the greedy men who rifled the packs and pockets of the dead men, and sometimes even the badly wounded. It had seemed shameful and depraved the first time he witnessed it. But that was days ago, and a lot had happened since then. Out here the logic was undeniable. What would become of the guns, the money, the clothes and personal effects, and even the body of a fallen and forgotten man like this? Nature and the beasts of the forest would claim everything Mel left behind.

As the draw he was following began to wind gently but steadily to the left, he realized that he was not only veering off in the wrong direction, but he was also lost in country a lot more rugged than he intended to pass through. There was more than one kind of lost, though, and Mel figured this wasn't the more serious kind where you scarcely know up from down, and began to feel like any direction you chose only took you farther and farther from where you wanted to be.

Good sense told him that all he had to do was find a manageable route up and over the steep rocky hill to his right, and then find a way to point his nose west again. In this country there was scarcely such a thing as traveling in a straight line, whether you went by river, road, or overland.

Struggling under the weight of his pack, nearly toppling backward a couple of times, and stopping often to catch his breath and rest the weary muscles of his arms, back and legs, it took Mel nearly half an hour to reach the crest. Ahead another draw awaited him, this one wider and flatter than the one behind. A swift, tumbling stream flowed down its middle two hundred feet below, splitting in spots to form small, brush-covered islands, then merging again beyond them.

Here was a possibility, Mel saw. If the stream was a tributary of the Little Bold River, as he suspected, and if its banks were passable, it could lead him back to known territory.

Making his way down the steep, broken rock face proved more difficult than climbing up had been. By the time he reached the bottom his palms and elbows were scratched and bleeding, and the knees and backside were nearly torn out of his britches.

Mel started downstream, making his way as best he could, walking sometimes on the wide sandy shoals and sometimes in the creek itself when the water was shallow and the footing was sure. In places the walls rose steep and rugged on either side, and in other stretches sheer limestone cliffs rose straight up a hundred feet or more. The place had a certain familiarity about it, and reminded him of other carefree times. He couldn't have sworn that he had ever been in this valley before, but if not, he had spent time in others like it.

As a half-grown boy, when the hardest of the spring farm-work was done and the crops were laid by for summer, Mel used to head out with his friend Pook for days at a time to hunt, explore, and live off the land. Pook was a Quapah Indian, two years Mel's senior, part of a dwindling band that had migrated here to the high country during the hottest summer months, probably for centuries.

He was just eleven that first summer when he asked to head out into the wilds for a few days with his friend. His mother was apoplectic at the thought of her only son striking out into the wilderness with a filthy, heathen Indian boy, carrying little more than a slab of bacon, cornbread, a hatchet, and a battered old single-shot twelve-gauge that nearly knocked him down every time he set it off.

After considerable debate, Daddy had overruled her, contending that it was good for a young man to go out exploring like that, to make it on his own and learn what the wild country had to teach him.

So he and Pook took to the woods that summer, and for the next few summers that followed. Each knew only a smattering of the other's language, but they managed to communicate, and became solid comrades over time.

Then one summer Pook never came strolling out of the woods in late May or early June, as Mel had grown accustomed to him doing every year. On inquiry, Mel's daddy had learned that the Quapah had not returned to the grassy meadow on the Little Bold where they traditionally set up camp in the summer months. It wasn't until sometime later that Mel learned that the Quapah were forced to leave their tribal lands in northern Arkansas, and had been relocated someplace out west. The news devastated him. Forlornly he still made his annual pilgrimage into the wilderness that year, but came home early and fell to work beside Daddy splitting cedar shakes for a shed roof. It wasn't the same.

The terrain he was following started to take on a steeper downhill slope. The creek began to tumble down from one rocky slab to another, making it impossible to wade along in its shallow waters. Mel's only choice was to scramble along through the heavy brush and tangled blackberry thickets that grew along the slanted banks. There were no game trails, and Mel figured that any deer or fox with half a brain avoided this place. Progress was slow and tiring.

When he reached a spot where part of the hillside had fallen away, leaving a flat ten-by-ten clearing beside the creek, he stopped and shrugged out of the heavy pack. The remainder of the deer shank in the pack was starting to put off a sour, unpleasant smell. It wouldn't be long before it became rancid and inedible.

He gathered a pile of leaves, sticks and deadfall and built a fire. He surrounded it with flat slabs of loose rock, then went to work on the deer meat as the rocks heated. He cut away the layers of spoiled and graying meat on the outside, then began to slice the fresher red meat inside into thin flat strips. Without salt and seasoning it wouldn't be the tastiest jerky he had ever produced, but it would do to fill the belly of a truly hungry man.

It took upwards of a couple of hours to dry all the deer meat worth saving. In the process he ate his fill, washing it down with water from the tumbling creek.

This was a nice spot, Mel thought. Under other circumstances it wouldn't be a bad place to spend the night. There was deadfall nearby for a fire, and plenty of fresh water an arm's length away. Few wild animals were likely to wander the steep hills nearby, and if any threat did arise, he had an arsenal to deal with it.

Then the realization came to Mel that he had spent the night here already, he and Pook, years before. They had been working their way up the valley, not down, and had been glad to find this level place to camp as darkness settled in. They had built their fire almost where his was now, and used it to cook beans in a blackened coffee can, along with a squirrel Mel had killed with his slingshot. Later a heavy rain began, and they spent the rest of the night huddled against the stone wall, as wet as minks, waiting miserably for daylight.

Slowly the whole night returned clearly to him, and with it came an oppressive loneliness and sense of loss. Not only were those carefree, adventurous boyhood days gone forever, but so was everything else that had shaped his world back then—Mother, Daddy, the house, the barn, the crops, the stock, the entire farm. If he died out here today—if he stumbled and drowned in the creek or if nature chose today to peel off another layer of granite from the sheer rock face above him—who would ever know, and who would mourn him? For the first time since all this madness started, he began to realize the completeness of his loss. It had taken Daddy many long years of hard labor to build that place up to the modest farm it had been, but only a handful of days were needed to turn it into little more than a cemetery. Could he ever rebuild it all? And even if he had the strength for the task, did he have the heart for the job?

In the midst of those moments of forlorn loneliness, another realization unexpectedly invaded his thoughts.

To reach this place, he and Pook had climbed up a steep rocky wall alongside a tumbling waterfall. And before they began the climb they had been working their way upstream along a river. He hadn't known the name of the river then, or really cared, but now he realized that it must have been the Little Bold. If his instincts were right, once he reached the river below, he would be back on track for the final leg of his journey to the Adderly farm.

His mood brightened like a lamp just lit, and the morose thoughts dissolved away. The past was past, and there wasn't time to grieve over losses right now.

He hurriedly gathered the last of the jerky into a cloth bag, then checked the loads of his rifle and pistols out of habit. He continued his descent of the steep hillside, climbing down hand-over-hand in some places as the creek spilled down the rock face beside him. When he reached the bottom, the creek became a creek again, flowing more slowly to the west. Somewhere up ahead, through the trees and brush on the valley floor, he heard the welcome sound of tumbling, rushing water.

The Little Bold, as Mel remembered it, was shallow and wide enough to ford in some places, but narrow, deep, and swift enough in other spots to sweep a man off his feet and carry him away. The water was clear and cold, and occasionally cascaded into rapids that tumbled over sheer rock shelves and funneled recklessly between jumbles of boulders. The banks were mostly forested right up to the water's edge, and there was a multitude of narrow, sandy, brush-infested islands that arose and then washed away at the whim of the river's currents.

When the heavy rains fell, usually in the spring, a river like this, flanked by steep hillsides, could become a raging, irresistible death trap. Sometimes the runoff from heavy rains could cause the water level to rise ten or twenty feet in a remarkably short time. The currents were strong enough to roll boulders over and uproot hundred-year-old trees. Caught up in waters like that, man and beast alike had to have God's own grace working for them to come out alive.

Mel half walked, half slid down a stretch of loose, gravelly dirt, and sat down on a log at the water's edge. He pulled off his shoes and put his feet in the river. The water was cold and soothing, and he reached down to splash refreshing handfuls up onto his head and chest.

Off to the left, a small rapid churned and tumbled down into a dark still pool directly out from where Mel sat. From time to time a bream or smallmouth would rise up with a splash to gobble some unlucky insect from the surface. Some other time one of them might end up as his supper, but not today.

After his short break he started downstream, wading across to the other bank when he came to a spot that was shallow enough. Once on the other side, he was surprised to discover what must have been an old logging road, now overgrown with weeds and shoulder-high seedlings. It was a welcome discovery because the remnants of the road would make for easier walking. If he was lucky, the road might even lead him close to the Adderly place.

Over the next hour he made encouraging progress, moving steadily toward his destination. When his stomach began to talk to him, he paused to eat a piece of the dried venison and take a long drink of river water. A chattery barking high up in an oak nearby caught his attention. He investigated the treetops for a few moments, and spotted a young squirrel crouched low on a limb, scolding a blue jay nearby.

Moving very slowly, trying not to call attention to himself, Mel retrieved his rifle and eased it up to his shoulder. The squirrel skittered off the limb and back out of sight on the opposite side of the thick trunk. Then it reappeared a few seconds later, ten feet lower on the trunk, and resumed its harassment of the jaybird. It was an easy shot and Mel's eyes followed the descent of the dead squirrel as it toppled down to the ground.

The fusillade of gunfire that answered his single shot could not have been more unexpected. It came from behind him, a dozen or more rifle shots back up the logging road in the direction he had come from. The shooters weren't close, and Mel figured they were firing blindly in his direction. But the mere fact that there were armed men, undoubtedly soldiers, out here in these deep woods, which had only a moment before seemed so vacant and still, sent a thrill of panic through him.

Where did they come from, and where were they going? They must be following the logging road. Maybe they had come across its starting point somewhere across the Gately Post Road and decided that it might be a shortcut to wherever they wanted to go.

Grabbing his pack and rifle, Mel waded out into the river, staying close to the bank and trying to be as quiet as possible. Within a hundred feet, he was in water up to his chest, struggling to keep the rifle and pack high and dry as he fought the power of the river current. Soon, near exhaustion, he lay his burdens up on the riverbank and clung to the low-hanging branch of a tree that leaned precariously out over the water.

The steep riverbank above him was overgrown with an impenetrable thatch of weeds, brambles and small willows. He thought he might be safe here unless they decided to search for him. In that case, he wouldn't be hard to find, and wouldn't be able to put up much of a fight in this predicament.

He heard them coming easily enough as they approached along the logging road somewhere on the other side of the brush and trees on the riverbank. There were a few horses, but no wagons. Most of the men seemed to be on foot, and they took no pains to be quiet as they tromped along. The men talked and grumbled in conversational tones, and occasionally a whiff of tobacco smoke reached Mel in his watery hideout.

It took a long time for all of them to move past. Mel had no way to guess how many there might be, or even what side they were on. Hundreds at least, probably more. As the last of them tromped by and the noise they made faded in the distance, the woods grew still again. He struggled up onto the bank, his feet and legs numb from the cold water. They were nearly useless for a while, but he rubbed some life back into them until he was able to struggle to his feet.

Mel backtracked down the logging road and easily located the squirrel he had killed. He settled on the ground with his back against the big oak to clean his kill and try to sort things out.

Wasn't there a single place in all this wild mountain country where he could avoid these soldiers and their damned nuisance of a war? he wondered.

He took off his clothes and wrung the river water out of them, then lay back naked in the sun to let it warm and dry his body. The inevitable happened, and he drifted off to sleep.

CHAPTER TEN

"Is he dead?"

"Don't appear to be. His color's good, and he don't look shot up enough."

Mel jolted awake. In an instant he had his rifle up and was looking around.

A few yards back down the road the two men he'd heard talking leaped into the trees on either side of the road. He heard one of them fall heavily and curse in pain.

"Damn it all, that shore didn't do my ankle no favor."

"Hey feller, don't be so jittery," a second voice called out. "We're stragglers, just like you."

Mel wasn't sure what to do. If he shot at them they were bound to shoot back, and the ruckus could alert the army that had passed not long ago. He could run off, but he'd have to take off naked because his clothes were scattered all about. And where could he run to anyway?

There didn't seem to be any threat in the voices he had heard.

A face peeked around a tree trunk. "Gave you a start, I s'pose," the man suggested. "But we're harmless enough. Oscar over there throwed his musket away some time back, and I ain't got more than a thimble full of powder left for mine."

"I think I'll need some help getting up over here, Bill," the second man called from somewhere off in the trees.

"A'right, I'll be there in a jiffy, Oscar. If this feller here don't mind."

Mel laid his rifle aside. It wasn't a time for fighting. "It ain't my affair," he said. "I don't own this road."

As the man behind the tree crossed over to help his friend up, Mel rose and quickly put his clothes back on. There was something about being naked that made a man feel downright vulnerable, even when he held a loaded rifle in his hand.

A minute later the three of them met up in the middle of the road.

"Oscar here twisted his ankle on a root," the one named Bill explained. "He couldn't keep up on the march, and I slipped back to watch out over him. He's my brother-in-law, and my sister back home would hold it against me if I lost him out here in these woods."

"We're sick of fighting anyway," Oscar added. "Five days now, and nothin' but one fight after another. If we show up late for the next one, I don't mind."

They were dressed in pieces and scraps of uniforms, and neither one looked like he'd had his fill to eat in weeks. Their beards were scraggly, and they both stank. The musket Bill carried was old and dirty, and Mel thought he'd hate to put it to his shoulder and try to shoot somebody.

"So what's your story?" Bill asked. "A man layin' bareassed naked out in the wilderness is bound to have a tale to tell." He had a vague crooked grin on his face, and struck Mel as the type that could find some scrap of humor in about any circumstance.

"I was filling my water bottle and fell in the river," Mel said. "I was going to dry out and catch up with the outfit, but I fell asleep under that tree." If he stayed around soldiers long enough, he thought he might become a passable liar.

"Well, if I was you, I wouldn't shilly-shally here too long," Bill counseled. "We figger the enemy ain't too far behind. Naked or dressed, it probably wouldn't go well for a man if they got their hands on him."

The two men started to move again. The one named Oscar hobbled along, suffering considerably each time he put his weight on his badly swollen ankle. He had a forked stick that he used as a crutch, and his brother-in-law helped some. With no better plan in mind, Mel fell in with them.

"We figure if we have the time we'll try to hide when we hear them comin' up behind us. And if we don't . . ." Oscar's voice trailed off without finishing.

"What I can't figure out is what we're doing out here in the deep woods anyway," Mel said. If they thought he was one of them, it wouldn't hurt to pretend he was, at least for now.

"I heard the blue bellies was waitin' for us up the post road someplace," Oscar said, "and had us bad outnumbered. So we took to the woods on this track. If we're lucky, we'll join up with General Willard and the main army up ahead."

"And if we're not lucky?" Mel asked.

"Then we try to make do for a spell on acorns and muscadines," Bill said.

The two men were well acquainted, and though they spent a lot of the time bickering over one unimportant thing or other, they were clearly fond of one another. Bill was very solicitous about Oscar's ankle, and insisted on frequent stops so Oscar could rest.

For his part, Mel considered ways that he might separate from this pair without causing suspicion. They might be eager to catch up with the army ahead, assuming it was their own, but Mel had no desire to fall in with either the one ahead or the one behind. The cliffs and hillsides on both sides of them were steep and forbidding, but he figured another hard climb was far better than finding himself in the middle of another battle.

"So what outfit you with?" Bill asked him.

"Fourth Arkansas, Major Elliot's bunch," Mel said, citing the only unit and officer that came to mind. He hoped that they didn't know Elliott, or at least didn't know he had been captured during the rout back at the farm.

"We're in the Fourth, too," Bill said. "Or at least what's left of it. We was under a little jackass named Turnipseed, but he ain't around no more. With all the fighting and moving around, I couldn't tell you who's in charge of the regiment no more."

"Don't s'pose it matters," Oscar mumbled.

Mel's thoughts went back to the moment he lined up his sights up on the middle of Turnipseed's shoulder blades and he began to squeeze the trigger. It was his belief that a man shouldn't take pride in a back-shooting, but that shot sure seemed right.

"I heard of Turnipseed," Mel said. "What happened to him?"

"Some think kilt, others say captured. But I got my own idea. I figure he skee-daddled back to Mama's teat when the air filled up with lead."

"Whatever happened," Oscar said, "good riddance to him, I say. I don't know what lamebrain came up with the notion that just 'cause a man's daddy has land and money, that makes him fit to lead fighting men. It's like you said, Bill. He wasn't nothin' but a jackass."

Mel would have liked to tell them that they had him to thank for putting a ball of lead into that particular jackass, and why, but he knew it wouldn't be a wise thing to do. There were bound to be rules against shooting officers, even the bad ones.

During their next stop Mel shared his jerky with the two men, and the one named Bill changed the dressing on Mel's wounds. It was a good thing because the nick on his shoulder was starting to turn red and oozy again. Infected and unattended, lesser wounds had cost men arms, legs, and even their lives.

They came across another group of stragglers in the middle

of the afternoon, men of a different ilk entirely. After one look at this bunch, Mel lowered his right hand and rested it on the hilt of his sidearm.

There were five of them, and the smallest man among them seemed to be calling the shots. There was immediate tension between them and the men Mel was traveling with when the little man explained that they'd had enough and were taking to the hills.

"Mama Hardisty didn't raise no cowards," he said. "But there was no fools in the litter, neither." That would be the excuse he'd live by in the years ahead, Mel suspected. Or maybe he'd turn himself into a war hero sometime down the road, and eventually start believing it himself.

He struck Mel as the kind of man who had spent his whole life getting by with big talk and bullshit, desperate to prove to himself and everyone else what a big man dwelled within his thin, undernourished frame.

"We done our own share of fighting, but this army is fallin' apart, and we don't see no use sticking around only to leave our bones to rot in these damn Missouri hollers. By dark we plan to be on top of that ridge up yonder," the man said, pointing up the steep hill beside them. "And tomorrow we point our peckers south."

"And what about when you get back home?" Bill asked.

"We heard they ain't doing nothing back home to the ones who decide to walk away. Hell, you boys oughter come on along. Our side's licked already, so what's the use?"

"I guess we'll see it through," Bill said, "but we don't fault you boys none for hightailing. It might end up the smartest thing." Hardisty and his bunch were all still armed with their muskets, and Mel figured Bill was talking so calmly to keep a fight from starting up. But he still stayed ready in case of trouble.

"I can't see why you want to climb up that durn mountain,

though," Oscar joined in. "Why not head back down this logging trace till you get to the post road?"

"We heered the blue bellies was back that way," one of the
five men said.

"Naw," Bill said, recognizing the deceit and playing along.
"Ain't nothin' back that way but whitetails and jackrabbits. But
if you fellers would rather climb up through the rocks and
brambles, it's no nevermind to me."

Every head turned toward the steep hillside beside the road.
Mel was glad he hadn't set his mind to climbing up it. Not unless it was his only chance of escape.

His companions went on their way as soon as they could.
Once they were out of earshot of the runaways, Bill began to
laugh. "Oscar, you got a mean streak," he said. "You know what
those men will run into if they head back down that road."

"Yeah, and I feel guilty as the devil about it," Oscar drawled.
"Maybe you oughta double back and let them know that they
are bound to run into the whole enemy army before they're
gone a mile."

"Maybe I will, then," Bill said, still grinning like a fool. "Let
me think on it."

About the time that the sun had dipped into the tops of the
trees to the west, they heard a rattle of musket and rifle fire up
ahead. It was only a few shots, and seemed far off. But Mel
knew that these winding valleys could do strange things with
sound.

"I thought the blue bellies was s'posed to be back of us, not
up ahead. What do you think?" Bill asked nobody in particular.
Neither of the other two had any immediate opinion. "Maybe a
skirmish is all," Bill said, answering his own question. "Maybe
they came on some runaways from the other side and lit into
them. Or maybe they met up with an enemy patrol."

They were still walking, but the uncertainty of what lay

ahead slowed their pace.

"Yeah, maybe," Oscar said without conviction.

Or maybe the two armies found each other again, Mel thought. Maybe those were the first shots of another big fight unfolding. In that case, these troops ahead, Bill's and Oscar's fellows, would be in desperate straits for sure, from one army ahead of them, and maybe another catching up behind.

Looking around him, Mel started to wonder how two armies would fight in rugged country like this. He'd seen how they did it in the woods and in the wide-open spaces back at his place, but how could two armies square off and have at each other in such narrow confines as this?

However they did it, he suspected that it would be a bloody, close-up tangle, and he had no hankering to be around to witness it. But where could he go? What could he do to stay out of it? Probably nothing.

A new ripple of gunfire began to crackle and pop up ahead, not steady and sustained yet like the gunfire Mel had witnessed in the battles at his farm, but growing toward it. The big guns had not started blasting yet. Some cannons had gone by while he hid at the edge of the river to let the army go by, but they probably wouldn't be much use in this mess. From what he had seen, they took a while to set up and load, and they were most useful at long range.

This fight was more likely to be face-to-face, man-to-man, and the devil take the loser.

"We need to get on up there and give our boys a hand," Oscar said. He was making a sad attempt to quicken his pace, and obviously paying the price in more pain.

"Peers they'll be needing us soon enough," Bill agreed.

"What help can you two be?" Mel asked, his voice containing more sarcasm than he had intended. "You don't even have anything to fight with no more."

"It's our fight," Oscar said, hobbling forward resolutely. "Mine, yours, and Bill's."

"And they'll soon be muskets enough to go around," Bill pointed out. "All Oscar will have to do is reach down and pick one up."

Mel wanted to announce then and there that he wasn't going with them. But something stopped him, something that didn't make a whole lot of sense. He barely knew these men, but he liked them, admired their loyalty and bravery, and he didn't want them to think bad of him. He didn't want them to lump him in with the likes of the cowards they had met back down the road.

So they pushed on, the three of them, hearts pounding in their throats, skittish as jackrabbits, to the unknown place not too far ahead where hundreds of men were facing off, killing and dying for reasons that not one in a hundred could probably explain.

The gunfire intensified, clearly much closer, no more than a few hundred yards now, he guessed.

Without warning they heard the sound of feet running toward them on the road, and moments later men began to appear around a bend at the foot of a hill. Mel and the others were barely able to get out of the way of the stampede. These were wild-eyed men, desperate and determined, focusing all their energy on escape now that they had learned a core truth about themselves.

Bill recognized one of the fleeing men and called out to him. "Joe! Joe Turner! What's going on up there? Is it lost? Are we whipped so soon?"

The man looked back at the sound of his name, but didn't stop running, and the look on his face told the story. He might do many brave things during the rest of his life, but the good in all of them would never erase the memory of this day. And then he ran square into a tree, a twelve-foot pine that grew up at the edge of the road. It knocked him silly but he didn't fall down. Blood began to flow from a deep gash in his forehead but he staggered on. Now you'll have a scar to help you remember today, Mel thought, and he wondered if he'd ever have the grit to tell anyone the truth of how he got it.

They continued forward as others fled the other way, sometimes alone, and other times in small bunches. Bill pointed out that there were always some who broke and ran, even during the battles they were winning. He retrieved muskets for himself and Oscar that others had cast off and checked their loads.

As for Mel, he didn't need any more guns. He carried a rifle and wore a holstered pistol at his waist. There were more handguns in his pack that the others didn't know about.

They were close. Not far up ahead, above the cracking din of gunfire, Mel began to hear the shouts and desperate screams and angry roars of men in battle. Bullets were whispering through the air around them, snipping leaves and thunking into tree trunks. He determined that he would advance no further. If he did, he would make himself a part of this.

Bill uttered a soft "uuh" sound as if someone had startled him. Mel turned in time to see the blossom of bright red blood on his shirt. Bill looked down at it too, then back up at Mel and Oscar, puzzled, as if he needed one of them to explain this mystery to him. Mel tried to catch him as he fell, but Bill's body had become dead weight and he crumpled awkwardly to the ground.

Oscar let out a wail, cast his makeshift crutch away, and fell on his knees beside his friend. "Bill! Oh Lordy, Bill. What have they done to you now?" He pulled his friend toward him and put his hand over the bloody patch on Bill's shirt, then lifted his hand and stared at the crimson blood incredulously.

Mel dropped to the ground by Oscar, mostly for safety. He didn't even bother to check Bill for signs of life. A bullet that dead-center in a man's chest could only have one result.

"He's dead now," Mel told Oscar urgently. "And we need to git." Oscar looked up at him as if he had spoken in some pagan tongue. Two men ran full tilt past them down the road, then half a dozen more followed. Only one that Mel saw still had a musket in his hands. A bullet sang by above their heads and slapped into a tree.

"There's no use going no further. You can't fight, and you can't run away with that leg of yours. But we can't stay here, either." When Mel took hold of Oscar's arm and pulled, Oscar shrugged away from him.

"We could wade out to that little island over there and hunker down in the brush," Mel said. "We might be okay there till this fight's passed us by."

Oscar seemed to be regaining some threads of coherence, and appeared to understand what Mel said. He looked up at Mel, then out to the narrow brush-covered island in the river, then back at Mel.

"We'll take Bill with us," Oscar said. "I have to take him home so we can bury him proper."

"We can't do that, there's no time," Mel insisted. "This fight is getting hotter, and it'll be right on top of us in a minute."

The flow of men hurrying back down the road was growing thicker, but there was a little different tone to the rampaging retreat. Occasional orders were shouted, and most of the men Mel saw now still had their muskets with them. These were the best, the ones who still had some fight left in them, even if they were losing badly.

"We'll come back for him," Mel said, knowing they never would. "After this is over." He manhandled Oscar to his feet and half steered, half dragged him to the riverbank.

The island was about thirty yards out, a long narrow knob of sand, rocks and soil, grown over with willows and brush too stubborn to be washed away in the spring floods. The current seemed manageable here and not too deep for wading. Mel lifted his rifle and pack high up with one hand, grabbed the back of Oscar's shirt with the other, and waded in. The noise, gunfire, and chaos crept relentlessly toward them. The road was jammed with men, so full that they spilled over into the river, some willingly and others by accident. Mel saw that he and Oscar were not the only ones seeking refuge on the island, but at this point they had no other choice.

The water grew deeper and the current more forceful than he expected. The stones under their feet were slippery with moss. Time and again Oscar's footing failed him and he went down, but each time Mel hauled him snorting and gagging back to the top.

"Ella ain't never gonna forgive me for leaving her brother laying dead like that," Oscar grieved. "He was the one supposed to be looking out for me. Not t'other way around."

The water was above their waists now, shoving at them insistently, determined to drag them under.

"Seems to me," Mel said, panting with the strain of his labors, "you should have stayed down there in Arkansas and lived your lives in peace."

"Maybe so. But all the neighbor men was joinin' up, so we did too."

The water was up to their armpits now and Mel was all but dragging Oscar forward. Back on the road, the pathetic force that must have constituted the rear guard was putting up a faltering defense, turning and firing, then trying to reload as they hurriedly withdrew again. Their numbers were dwindling fast.

Mel caught his first glimpse of the other side, recognizing

them by the sight of their blue uniforms through the brush and trees. They advanced in no particular hurry, moving from tree to tree or rock to rock, taking a shot when they had one and then ducking down to reload.

Mel realized that he and Oscar had to get out of the water in a hurry and find some cover. Out here in midstream they were easy targets.

Out of the corner of his eye he saw a man not far upstream step into a hole and go under. He surged to the surface seconds later, gasping in a desperate appeal for help, and sank under again. But the current had him, sweeping and tumbling him along and never letting go. The next time he came up he was a few feet upstream from Mel and Oscar. He groped out desperately for salvation, but all he succeeded in doing was snatching Oscar out of Mel's grasp. In one startling instant Mel watched the two men roll under the surface and stay there. He thought he saw their bodies tumble into a rapid on downstream, but it was hard to tell.

Mel struggled on, the going much easier now without his burden, until he reached the island and threw himself on a gravel bar. A bullet chewed up a patch of gravel near him, and he crawled forward into a jumble of dead trees deposited there by one flood or another. Secure for the moment in the tangle of dead roots, branches, and fractured timber, he lay still and tried to think things through. The fight had moved on south along the logging road and on to God only knew where. He didn't really care where they decided to fight, as long as it wasn't right on top of him. Again.

Mel had seen other refugees head toward the island earlier. Although he couldn't see any of them at the moment, he felt certain that some were still close by. Their mere presence there made the place unsafe for him to stay for long.

He had lost the rifle someplace, but didn't recall where. Probably in the river. He still had the holster around his waist and the guns and the pack, but everything was soaked and the stock of gunpowder would be ruined. He, Bill, and Oscar had finished the last of his food earlier in the day.

It was dusk now, and Mel welcomed the arrival of night. The fighting had pushed farther south, back in the direction he and his now-dead companions had come from earlier. The shooting was more random than it had been earlier—desperate spates of gunfire, followed by tense periods when only the gurgling of the river and the chorus of the nighttime frogs and insects could be heard.

Mel pictured the scene somewhere up the valley where the retreating Arkansans must be fighting for their survival right now, not in any organized way, but in small desperate packs, and even one by one, with no real hope of making it out of this place alive.

What amazed him most was the ruthlessness and hatred with which these men had at each other. Were the causes they fought for so important as that? Or was it something else, something so deep down in them that they really didn't understand it themselves?

Sometimes the wild creatures in the forest fought to the death for no reason that any outsider could understand. And sometimes, apparently, so did men.

Exhausted, Mel dozed off on the sand and gravel bed where he lay, satisfied that he was at least partially hidden by the tangle of wood and brush around him. It wasn't a restful sleep because the fading gunfire roused him from time to time, as did snippets of disturbing dreams. Rochelle drifted in and out of the dreams, always at risk, always searching for him. Bill and Oscar were there too, pestering him in a good-humored but persistent way, insisting that he get their corpses back on home. "Ella's already got the graves dug," Bill insisted. "She's gonna be mad as a yellow-jacket if you don't get us back there to go in 'em."

When it was as dark as it was likely to get, Mel snaked out from under the driftwood pile and stood up. His knees and hips were stiff, but otherwise he felt pretty good. It was quiet all around except for the eternal rippling of the river. Even the distant gunfire had stopped. He could see very little around him, but the river gave him his bearings.

Shouldering his wet pack of guns and necessities, he waded back into the water, feeling his way along a step at a time. He used the press of the river current against his legs to keep them moving in the right direction, and eventually began to make out the dim outline of the opposite bank. Even in the pitch dark, it was a much easier crossing than before, when he was forced to drag a crippled man along behind him in the midst of a running battle.

Staggering up out of the water, he came almost immediately upon two dead bodies at the edge of the logging road. One of their muskets lay close by, but the stock was broken and he didn't bother retrieving it. His most pressing need at the moment was dry powder and he found a sufficient stock of it in the leather boxes each of the dead men wore on their belts.

Mel settled on the ground beside the bodies and begin taking apart the pistol still strapped to his waist. It was a tricky operation in the dark, disassembling, cleaning, and loading a gun he was not familiar with, but it was important to have at least one of the weapons he carried ready to fire again. This was no place to be walking around unarmed.

He regretted the loss of the rifle he had been carrying. By his reckoning, it was one of the best he had ever seen in use in any of these battles, better than anything he had ever owned or could reasonably aspire to own. But he would remember the spot, and one day he could come back and spend whatever time he needed to find it.

When he thought about it, he realized that this whole valley would probably be littered with relics and remnants of the running fight that was fought here. At his farm, both armies had done their best to get the dead underground where they belonged, and to gather up the weapons and gear the dead had left behind. But here they seemed to have moved on already. How likely was it that either bunch would ever send anyone back to tidy up this remote and easily forgotten battlefield?

There were things of value all about here, especially the firearms, which could be sold to pay for the lumber and other material and tools needed to rebuild his farm.

But that would have to be done later, assuming of course that the story of his life had a "later" connected to it.

He considered cleaning and charging the other handguns in his pack, but decided against it. It would be a difficult and time-consuming effort, and when he was finished, he would still have to put them back in the wet pack. So what was the use?

The faint spackling of light he spotted through the trees and brush to the north had an eerie quality to it. His first thought was of the Indian legends and folktales about this ghost or that, perpetually searching for one thing or another that had been meaningful to them in life. As he remembered the tales, most of them carried lights, even the headless ones.

If such things were possible, there certainly could be a lot of ghosts wandering these parts tonight. As a cold chill spread over his skin at the mere thought of it, he fought down a rush of mindless animal panic. There was no place to go, no place safe to hide, so if ghosts were afoot tonight, he would just have to deal with them, or perish in whatever gruesome way they deemed fit for him.

A second light joined the first in the distance. They were obviously coming down the road in his direction. Mel quietly withdrew to a thicket of weeds and brush several feet off the road and settled in to let them pass.

When he began to hear the cautious tone of the conversation, Mel was convinced that these were men and not specters. Surely ghosts would not curse the darkness with such foul language. They were probably soldiers, separated during the fighting, trying to rejoin whatever army they belong to.

"Look yonder. There's a couple."

Although Mel could not see the group clearly, there seemed to be four or five of them, two leading the way with lanterns, and the rest stumbling along behind in the shadows.

"These here is mine," one of the intruders announced, moving ahead of the others with his light.

"Hell, it don't make no difference, does it? We all agreed to divide everything fair in the morning."

"That was fine till I seen Luke slip something in his shirt back at that last bunch."

"It wasn't nothing. A hunk of bread is all. I showed it to you."

"Yeah, that's what you showed me, all right."

When they reached the two dead men they knelt around them like feeding buzzards, and fell to work. Mel remained still as they set to their task, emptying pockets and stripping the dead men of shoes, socks, shirts, and trousers. One of the scroungers stripped off his own tattered shirt and threw it to the side, then pulled on the shirt belonging to one of the dead soldiers.

They stuffed their sorry treasures in the burlap sacks they carried, then stood and moved on down the road. They went no more than one hundred feet before finding more dead bodies, and repeating their shameful routine.

How many more men like this would be wandering the woods tonight? Mel wondered. Was it like this after every battle? Dying out here in the wilderness was indignity enough, but there was something particularly disgraceful about having your corpse stripped naked by fools like these. True, Mel had stolen from the corpses too, but he had taken only what he needed to survive. He hadn't made a business of it, which he strove to believe set him well apart from these hounds.

The night was a long and jittery one as Mel worked his way cautiously north along the old logging road. The moon rose eventually, making it easier to see his route—but also making him more easily seen. He skirted a camp where several men lay asleep on the bare ground near a dying campfire, and hid from another small band of scavengers. The river valley widened and the hillsides on either side became less steep and forbidding. He had passed well beyond the area where the fighting had been, and there were no more bodies laying about.

Where the road crossed the river at a wide shallow ford, he came to a patch of cleared land, a farm place long abandoned. The cabin and a couple of outbuildings still stood, though none were in good shape. It appeared that several hundred men had made their camp here recently.

Mel entered the cabin cautiously, his pistol drawn, but no one was inside. He stretched out on the hard dirt floor and fell almost immediately asleep. He was so spent that he hardly gave a thought to what might happen if someone found him resting here.

Chapter Eleven

The next day dawned so clear and pretty that any man who had not been through what Mel Carroll had in the past few days might easily forget about the fighting and killing that raged all over these parts. But Mel hadn't forgotten, not just yet, and he took a careful look around through one of the cabin windows before venturing outside. There was nobody about, living or dead, and he figured he must have walked out of the killing zone sometime during the night.

He washed his face and hands in the cold refreshing water of the Little Bold River. He was tempted to strip down and take an all-over bath, but the thought of someone happening along and again catching him bare naked and unarmed put a stop to that idea.

He shot a ten-inch turtle sunning on a log and soon had several strips of turtle meat roasting over a small fire. Ordinarily turtle wasn't one of his favorites, especially smoky and charred as this would be, but today the odor of the roasting meat made him ravenous. He couldn't remember the last time his belly had been full to the point of satisfaction.

While his breakfast cooked, he cleaned and reloaded all the handguns in his small arsenal. Besides the biggest and best, which he wore in a holster, there were three pretty-good ones in the pack as well as a couple of sorrier ones that didn't look like they would be trustworthy in a bad situation.

Mel now had a sound reckoning of where he was, and after

his turtle meat breakfast, he set off north at a brisk pace. There was plenty of evidence that an army had passed this way, but no signs of any fighting in this area. Missing as well was the distant, unsettling sound of gunfire. Perhaps the war finally moved on out of their little remote corner of the state, and folks hereabouts could start putting things back in order. But he had thought that before, only to be caught up again in the fighting.

It was too much to hope that the Adderlys and their home place had escaped the turmoil and destruction, but maybe old Ezekiel had been able to take his family away before the fighting started. If that was so, and if the armies had truly moved on, then maybe they would have returned by now to see how bad things were and to figure out what to do with what was left.

At any rate, he'd find out soon, probably before the sun reached the midday sky.

The valley where the Adderly place was located was still heavily wooded with old-growth hardwood at its upper end, but Ezekiel and his sons had cleared much of the lower end by the river, turning it into fields and pasture. The cabin, barn, and outbuildings were at the far end of the valley, high up enough from the river to avoid the spring overflows, tucked back into a grove of oak, birch, elm and chestnut. It was a pretty little spread, well tended and even more remote than Mel's own place.

But clearly the farm was not remote enough to have escaped the same fate as his. All the signs were there—the wrecked fences, destroyed fields, the barricades and earthen berms lining the river, and the crooked rows of hastily dug graves in what had been a pasture. Even from a distance Mel could see that the barn was down, and he guessed the house was too, burned down or blown apart by the cannons.

There was not a living creature in sight, no farm animals, no soldiers, and certainly no members of the Adderly family. Mel felt the hollow dread growing in him as he trudged down the valley toward the deserted battleground.

His fears were confirmed as he approached the grove where the Adderly home had stood. A blackened stone chimney stood sentinel over a shamble of ashes and debris. Smoke still drifted up from the long walnut foundation logs on which Ezekiel had built his family's home. They looked to have been smoldering for days.

The barn, a hundred yards farther away, was demolished and down. The whole area had the look of a place that had been swept by the hand of chaos. And indeed it had.

Mel had no idea what to do, or even what to think, about what he was now seeing. For days his mind had been set on simply making it here, on finding Rochelle and doing what he could to help her family. Beyond that he'd only entertained vague thoughts about letting her know his intentions, about staying around to give what help he could, and eventually starting over back at his place with the little that was left.

It could take days or weeks to find them now, if they had survived and if, unlike him, they had made the smart decision to leave before the fighting started. There were other farms in the area, a dozen or more at least within a few hours' ride. Surely they wouldn't all have suffered the same destruction, and surely any of them would take in old Ezekiel and his brood. Cable Springs was no more than twenty miles on up the post road, and they might have fled there instead.

Or, Mel thought, gazing with dread at the new graveyard in the pasture, they might be there, buried anonymously with the hundreds of men who had traveled to this place to fight and die. Mel felt hollow inside when he considered the possibility that he might never see any of them again, and might never know what happened to the woman he hoped to make his wife.

He wandered the Adderly place for a while, surveying the

damage, looking for anything that might be salvaged, and cataloging in his mind what would need to be done first to begin putting the place back in order if anyone survived to do the work. One small cornfield, the one furthest from the fighting, seemed to have remained undisturbed. That would make a meager crop for meal and feed—if any people and livestock remained to eat it. Many of the fences were down, but a few days' work would remedy that. The barn was flat but hadn't burned, so much of its timber could be used to build a new one.

He was on his way up to the barn to take a closer look when the soft sound of a woman's voice beneath the rubble stopped him short. In a moment a disheveled figure scrambled out into the open and rose stiffly to its feet. It was a woman, obviously, wearing a long dark skirt, a shapeless shirt, and a man's felt hat crammed down over unkempt hair.

"Chick, chick, chick. Chiiiick, chick, chick."

Mel realized it was Mrs. Adderly, though he scarcely recognized her. With one hand she held her apron gathered together in front of her.

"Chiiiick, chick, chick."

Two scrawny chickens appeared from someplace and started toward her, expecting to be fed by this familiar figure. She reached into the apron with her free hand and dropped a few grains of corn on the ground at her feet. The chickens immediately went to work on it.

In a smooth, practiced move, Mrs. Adderly reached down and closed her hand over one chicken's head. She lifted the chicken to her side and gave it a couple of deft swirls in the air. The chicken dropped to the ground and went running frantically away, blood spouting from the hole where its head had been. But it didn't get far before falling over and twitching in its death throes. The other chicken continued to eat greedily. More for her, until her own turn came.

"Mrs. Adderly? Henrietta Adderly?" Mel said, not speaking too loud so he wouldn't shock her.

The woman turned toward him, stumbling and nearly falling in her surprise. She looked filthy, ancient, and ill-used, like a hundred-year-old crone, although Mel knew she was not much past fifty, if that.

"It's Melvin Carroll, ma'am," Mel said softly. "Your neighbor." Her eyes looked wild and confused, so he added, "You don't have to be afraid. I've come to help." As if to demonstrate his good intentions he walked over and picked up the dead chicken by its feet.

"That's my chicken!" The woman said in alarm. "Please, we haven't had nothin' since yesterday."

Mel took the chicken over and gave it to her. "Do you recognize me? Melvin Carroll, from over east of here?" There was a look on her face that disturbed him. It was not quite madness, but something closely akin. Whatever had happened here had clearly taken her beyond the point of reasonable sense and reality.

"Melvin . . . That boy . . . Rochelle," she said, wrestling with her scattered thoughts but not quite able to piece them together. "My husband is obliged to have a talk with you, boy."

"Where are they, Henrietta? Your husband and Rochelle and the others? Are you here alone?"

The woman's face seemed to change shades, as if a heavy gray cloud passed between her and the sun. Her eyes bore a look unlike any Mel had ever seen before. There was terror there, and emptiness, and despair. She's near the abyss now, he thought. It won't take much more to send her over.

"Henrietta? Are you there, missus?" It was Ezekiel Adderly's voice, weak and raspy, but his all right, coming from somewhere beneath the rubble of the barn. "Come on back now, sugar.

Don't stray too far out there or you'll get yourself lost."

Mel saw the worn place in the dirt where she had been crawling in and out beneath the fallen timbers and planks. He walked over to the spot and called out, "Mister Ezekiel, it's me, Mel Carroll. I come to help."

"Henrietta, come on back now. It's okay, you can get a chicken later."

Ezekiel Adderly spoke as if he hadn't heard Mel at all, which puzzled Mel because they were only a few feet apart.

Mrs. Adderly brushed by Mel, dropping to her hands and knees, and crawled into the shadowy opening, dragging the dead chicken along through the dirt. "Ah, so you did find one then," Ezekiel Adderly proclaimed from inside. "Praise the Lord, at least for that small blessing."

"Mister Ezekiel, it's Mel. I'm coming in," Mel called out. There was no answer.

A mix of foul odors met Mel as he wormed into the tangle of fallen lumber. Worse than the stench of filthy bodies and human waste was something even more foul, which Mel easily recognized as the odor of decay and death. There must be dead bodies under these ruins, bodies that the advancing army hadn't taken the time to uncover and bury.

The opening widened after a few feet, and Mel stopped in surprise at what he saw ahead. The Adderlys had set up a little nest for themselves in space left open by chance when the barn collapsed. It was about five feet wide and eight feet long, formed by a span of rafters that had fallen across the side planks of a stall. There was headroom enough to sit up comfortably, but not quite enough to stand.

Ezekiel Adderly lay flat on his back on one side of the open space, unmoving and utterly wretched. Mel might have taken him for dead if he hadn't heard him speak a moment before. He was bare to the waist, and all that remained of his trousers were filthy tatters. His right leg was swollen to twice its normal size, a hideous, blackened, unnatural thing that oozed pus and body fluids from a ragged hole midway on his thigh.

Mel realized that what he smelled as he crawled in was undoubtedly his neighbor's rotting leg.

Henrietta Adderly was off in a corner pulling feathers off the chicken, her back to Mel, so for a moment his presence was unnoticed.

"Lord Almighty," Mel mumbled. "I would have tried to get here sooner if I knew things were so bad."

Ezekiel Adderly blinked his eyes a couple of times but didn't move his head. His eyes were fixed on a spot above him. The muscles of his face worked in twisted grimmaces, no doubt trying to keep a host of agonies at bay. Mel couldn't even imagine the depths of pain that a rotting leg like that must cause.

"They took Ham on off with them," the old woman said unexpectedly. She didn't turn her head toward Mel, and he was struck with the odd notion that she seemed to be explaining her son's plight to the chicken. "Said they'd make a soldier of him. My little Ham. My little gravy-eater."

The Adderlys had four offspring, two sons and two daughters. The oldest, Jaipeth, had left over a year before to fight, and months at a time had passed with no news of him. The younger son, Ham, who would be about sixteen now, was a lean, solid youth, quiet to a fault, and hardworking. It was hard for Mel to picture him running up a hillside with a musket in his hands, ready to kill some fellow from Arkansas.

"What about the girls, Miss Henrietta?" Mel asked quietly. He felt ashamed for showing his concern for Rochelle, with these two here in the shape they were, but the honest truth was that she was the reason he had come. "Where's Rochelle and Becky?" There was no answer from the girls' mother. The chicken held her attention.

Mel crawled forward and touched Ezekiel Adderly's arm, then shook it lightly. The old man blinked and cocked his head slightly to the side. Tears trickled out of the corners of his eyes and ran down his cheeks into his beard. His ears were crusted with rivulets of dried blood.

"Who are you?" Ezekiel asked.

"It's Melvin Carroll, sir," Mel told him. "I'm so sorry. I would have come sooner if I knew how bad things were here."

"You're not one of them . . ." The old man's eyes searched Mel's features, and a glimmer of recognition came to them. "Wait, I know you. You're that Carroll boy, aren't you?"

"Yes, sir. I'm Mel."

"Before all this I was coming after you soon as my mare foaled." His eyes darkened and Mel was put on his guard. "I only learned last week what you done to my girl, my Rochelle, and I was coming for you." Even now, in this place and this condition, a flash of anger and outrage still lit the old man's face, but the pain and misery soon drove it away.

For his part, Mel hung his head, feeling a sudden, unexpected shame that had not troubled him since that night with Rochelle at the dance weeks ago. But how could he explain to this man, who was the girl's father, who could not hear, and who was almost dead, that he had fought all the way over here to do the right thing by his daughter?

"Them caves is drafty and damp and full of bats," Henrietta told the dead chicken a few feet away. She was cutting the bird up and dropping the pieces into a dented pot, although her plucking job was hardly perfect. Mel couldn't figure out where or how she planned to cook it.

"Maybe you can carry on thataway with some of them girls from town, boy, but my Rochelle's a God-fearing and decent . . . ," Ezekiel said.

"It's not a fit place for no young girls." This from Henrietta.

"You need to remember the Lord's got his eye on you all the time, boy. He seen what you done, and I'm sure it broke his heart, same as it did her mama's and mine."

"They oughtn't to take my babies off to no caves like that. Those were black-hearted men, sent by Satan, that last bunch was."

Suddenly Mel stopped listening to the old man's reproaches, although his sermon continued in halting gasps.

"Who took the girls, Miss Henrietta?" Mel blurted out. "Was it after the army left? Was it deserters?"

Henrietta Adderly looked over at Mel, and he could see in her eyes that her addled brain was trying to make some sense of his presence here, and perhaps all the rest. "We wasn't expecting company for dinner," she said. "We don't have much."

"It's all right, ma'am. I'm not hungry. Tell me about the girls. Did some bad men take them to the caves?"

"Them bats can make you sick, you know. Even the guana can. It does wonders for tomatoes and cucumbers and squash. But you got to be careful how you handle it, same as chitterlings, and wash up after with some strong lye soap. It'll make you throw up like a buzzard."

"How long ago was it, Miss Henrietta?" Mel asked urgently. Frustrated, he wanted to shake the information out of the addled old woman. But that wouldn't work. Her brain was too mixed up already. Her thoughts seem to flitter around from one thing to the next like a mosquito.

"They kept coming and coming, like the armies of David, and during the fight they killed my husband Zeke. Might near. When they moved on they took almost everythin' we had, including my boy Ham. And when that last bunch come they took the little bit we had left. Took my girls too, and them crying and begging and fighting whilst they was drug off."

"I'm so sorry, Miss Henrietta," Mel said quietly, stroking her dirty wrinkled hand.

"They was three chickens that ran away in the bushes. We ate one yesterday, and now this one."

Henrietta Adderly turned away from Mel and lay flat on the ground in front of the low entrance to their little den. She crawled out awkwardly, dragging the pot of raw chicken along with her.

Mel considered what she had told him. After the main army left, some other men, the "black-hearted" ones, came along to scavenge whatever they could, including Rochelle and her younger sister. They must have mentioned caves in front of Henrietta, which would be an ideal place for them to hide out until the armies cleared out of the area. And with one chicken cooked yesterday, and one in the pot today, that meant one or two days had passed since they were here.

That was time enough to do some pretty awful things to two young girls.

His thoughts were interrupted when Ezekiel Adderly moaned out in sudden pain. His face was gray, his features contorted with inexpressible suffering. His lips moved silently as if he was praying, which he probably was. Mel could see the black lines of infection and decay creeping up his bare belly, and wondered how he had managed to live this long.

The humane thing to do would be to end his suffering now. But he could not bring himself to do that any more than he could end his own father's life during those final agonizing days on earth. Suddenly Ezekiel Adderly flung his hand out, and his work-roughened fingers locked around Mel's wrist. Mel endured the pain of the old man's iron grip and allowed himself to be pulled close.

"Melvin Carroll, you must be my blood avenger," Ezekiel said in a pulpit voice filled unexpectedly with righteousness and authority.

"I don't know what that means," Mel admitted uncomfortably, although he knew the old man wouldn't hear his words.

"In the Lord God Jehovah's almighty and righteous name," Ezekiel proclaimed, "I give you holy commission to do for me what I cannot do for myself." The rush of strength and will required to make that high-sounding proclamation took its toll. Ezekiel's grip on Mel's arm weakened and his hand fell away. His eyes drifted closed, and the breath left his body in a prolonged hiss.

Mel sat there for a moment, thinking he had witnessed his neighbor's last seconds of life. But then, eventually, Ezekiel's chest rose slightly, taking in new air, then hissing it back out again. Ezekiel Adderly's time wasn't up, not quite yet, which was probably unfortunate for him in many ways.

Mel crawled back outside and sat for a moment to let his eyes adjust to the midday brightness. What the devil was a "blood avenger" he wondered. Knowing old Ezekiel's religious bent, it probably had something to do with olden Bible days, but he didn't know the scriptures well enough to sort it out.

A few yards away, Henrietta Adderly had built a fire inside a circle of stones, and was on her way down to the river to fill the cooking pot with water. Her wits might have gone completely queer on her because of everything that had happened to her family, but the practices of a lifetime still guided her.

Mel knew he had to find the girls quickly, but his conscience wouldn't let him walk away and leave these two people, neighbors and friends of his family for much of his life, in such a sad state. There was one more chicken left for tomorrow and that was it for them unless he helped them out. There wasn't much left in the family's garden, but after scraping around in the dirt with a board for half an hour, he managed to dig up several sweet potatoes and turnips. There were a few green apples in the upper branches of the family's apple trees that the soldiers managed to overlook. Mel hacked the branches free and let them fall to the ground, then picked a bucket full of the hard immature two-inch fruits.

There were blackberries aplenty in the thickets at the edge of the woods, and while picking them, he also managed to shoot a young rabbit that had ventured out into the edge of the field. All these simple provisions he stockpiled by the entrance to the Adderlys' nest under the fallen-down barn.

Henrietta Adderly had long since taken the boiled chicken back inside, but she could hardly miss the provisions he had gathered when she came back out. Mel thought about crawling back inside to tell them where he was headed and what he planned to do, but he saw no real use in it. Henrietta wouldn't understand a word he said, and Ezekiel had already given him his marching orders. The day was more than half gone already, and there was no time to spare.

He found an old lantern alongside the barn which still contained enough oil to serve his purposes. After checking it and shouldering his pack of armaments, he started away with long urgent strides toward the rugged hill country which lay close by to the Adderly farm.

Chapter Twelve

Mel knew where to look. Northwest of the Adderly farm there was a steep, narrow gorge called Meat Holler, named for the fact that any hunter who ventured up that way was likely to return home with fresh game. There were two caves up in Meat Holler, both toward the upper end. One was a large, gaping hole in the side of a mountain, visible from a long way off, dark and foreboding like the mouth of hell. The other, farther along, looked like nothing more than a three-foot-wide split in the solid rock face. But anyone who ventured deep enough in discovered that, after a dozen yards or so, the gap widened, the floor leveled, and its dark passageways probed deep inside the mountainside.

During his boyhood Mel had explored the caves a few times with Jaipeth, the older Adderly boy, and other friends, usually probing into the big cave only a few hundred feet, no farther than the daylight permitted. But it was with his Indian friend Pook that the reckless daring of adolescence nearly led to both their deaths. The two of them decided that it would be their quest to confirm the legend that the two caves were actually separate entrances to the same underground system. Unwisely using bundles of burning brush as torches they recklessly explored deep into the larger opening, heedless of the fact that they would need light to find their way out as well as in. When their torches burned out, they might have easily become two wretched skeletons waiting to be found someday by future adventurers.

Mel still remembered the terrifying feeling of being lost in the utter darkness, completely disoriented, never knowing whether the next step would plunge him into a bottomless chasm or leave him facing a solid stone wall. For a long time they had yelled like maniacs for help, knowing the whole time that there was not another soul within miles, and certainly no one else in the cave, to hear their cries.

Only the calm thoughtfulness of his friend eventually saved them. After what seemed like hours of aimless wandering, they begin to hear the fluttering and squeaking of the bats far off in the distance, and they stumbled in that direction. When the sound stopped, so did they.

"Night go out, day in," Pook had explained. "We wait. Show us."

Countless harrowing hours passed in the numbing darkness between the bat flights. They slept when they could and Pook frequently passed the time chanting quietly under his breath. Mel didn't understand the words, but decided it was his friend's way of praying to whatever gods his tribe held sacred. Mel spent his own share of time praying to his Almighty, making promises of honesty and charity and clean wholesome living if only God would send his angels to lead them out of this mess. They had no food but there was water enough in the shallow puddles on the cave floor. They found them by touch, and lapped the water up like dogs.

After three maddening days and nights, the young Indian's simple logic had worked for them. The bats guided them to the narrow upper cave entrance, to fresh air and open spaces, to wonderful, glorious daylight.

Well before he came in sight of the lower cave entrance, Mel realize that the old woman had been right. He knew there were men there because he could smell their fire. As he crept closer, he could hear them moving around inside and talking from time to time. When he had moved as close as he dared, Mel crouched in the brush for a long time, listening and watching. There were several of them, he couldn't tell how many, but ten or more he thought. They were preparing for the approaching night, dragging in deadfall for their watch fires, and cooking slabs of venison cut from a carcass that lay in the dirt near the cave's mouth.

There was no sign of the Adderly girls, and no mention of them in the scraps of conversation he overheard. It was possible that Rochelle and her sister weren't even here, Mel realized.

But Henrietta Adderly had talked about the caves. She must have heard those men mention caves when they came to pillage the farm and carry off her daughters, and these were the only caves that Mel knew of for miles around. If Rochelle and her sister were here, they were probably somewhere deep inside where they couldn't run off.

Mel considered possibilities. He could pretend to be a straggler himself and try to join up. But they might decide it was easier to kill him and steal what he had than to take him into their band. Or he might wait until late at night and try to slip in. But wouldn't a pack of runaway soldiers be likely to post guards? He could fight his way in, but how would that work if he wasn't able to kill all of them? The second he fell they'd finish him off, and Rochelle and Becky's last hope for salvation would be gone.

Only one other way seemed open to him. He'd have to try the upper entrance, if he could find it in this failing light after so many years.

Far off to the southeast Mel heard a series of distant rumbles which he no longer mistook for thunder. He wondered briefly what little scrap of land they were fighting over now, and how many more men would be planted in the ground of a battlefield that would only be abandoned tomorrow.

Judging by the direction and distance, they may have even turned back to complete the destruction of what little was left of his own farm. He hoped someone would take the time to bury the dead like they had before. The idea of returning to a home place littered with mutilated, rotting corpses made him feel like his skin was crawling with spiders.

He had trouble finding the upper cave entrance. Years had passed since he was in these parts and there were plenty of similar clefts in the rocks to confuse a man. But the bats came to his aid once again. As night fell, they poured out in a fluttering, eerie, squeaking cloud, seeming to appear like magic from the vertical stone wall of the mountain. Mel stayed well clear until the last stragglers had made their exit.

As he neared the cleft in the rock he felt the perpetual rush of cool damp air, sucked in through the lower entrance and forced out here through this narrow opening. It bore familiar smells remembered from his youth—mustiness and decay, and the ammonia tinge of centuries of accumulated bat guano. But there was another smell on the breeze as well, the smell of wood smoke from the deserters' fires. That smell would guide him to where he needed to go.

Once inside he lit the lantern and looked around. Nothing seemed familiar. There was nothing there that resembled a floor. He had to scramble over piles of stone rubble, and step across chasms that would surely be bone-breakers if a man fell into one of them. After a few dozen yards he shrugged out of the heavy pack and left it behind, taking along only one handgun in the holster and another tucked in his belt.

Even when the rushing air diminished, he realized that the flicker of the lantern's flame would show him which way the air was moving, and which way he should head.

Before long Mel reached a massive chamber, so large that the weak light of the lantern didn't reach the other side or the towering ceiling somewhere far above. In the center of the chamber was a jumbled mass of broken stone at least fifty feet high. Away in the distance somewhere he heard the rushing sound of an underground waterfall. This was a place he did remember vaguely because he and Pook had the devil of a time working their way around the huge pile of fallen stone in total darkness. The lantern made the job a lot easier this time.

On the other side of the enormous rock pile, the vertical stone wall was split by cracks and openings of all sizes and descriptions, and none seemed familiar. Again he relied on the lantern and his own nose to find the way.

The air and the smell of smoke came out from between two flat layers of rock with about three feet of clearance between them, showing him the way. This was the long crawl that he remembered clearly, and dreaded most, when he thought about returning to the caves. As a careless teenage boy it had taken all the courage he could muster to go down on hands and knees and start that long, terrible crawl to who-knew-where.

Now as a grown man, and with the added advantage of light that the lamp provided, he still found the prospect of this crawl between the slabs of stone nearly impossible to face. Horrible images of the two stone layers slamming suddenly together entered his head uninvited. In an instant muscle, flesh, organs and bone would be flattened into a bloody mess no more than a tiny fraction of an inch thick, and for all time, no one would ever know, and few enough would probably even wonder, what had become of him.

But Rochelle was on the other side, and this seemed the only way to reach her.

As he moved forward, the space between the two rock slabs began to narrow until, for a time, he was scooting along on his belly like a reptile. His elbows and knees were scraped raw, and the muscles of his arms, neck, back and legs were on fire. He kept the lamp ahead of him, inching it along carefully, fearfully aware that that flickering flame embodied his only hope of making it back to the surface of the earth alive.

During those torturous minutes, fresh air, open sky, and blessed sunlight seemed like the most precious of all God's gifts to humankind.

Images of when he was buried alive under the dead soldier a few days before began to creep uninvited into his thoughts, and with them came the same desperate animal panic he had felt in the mass grave as the dirt began to cover him.

The clammy, damp stink of fear was all over him, and the strength and will seemed to drain from his cramped muscles. A man could easily slip into madness in a place like this, Mel thought, and it wouldn't take long.

Then in tantalizing slowness, the crawl space began to increase in height until at last he was back up on his hands and knees, moving at least like a dog now instead of a snake or a lizard. Then eventually he was back on his feet again, as a man should be. The tension began to drain away as his muscles and joints limbered, and he tried not to think about the fact that he might soon be facing that same awful crawl going back. But if he had to do it again, at least he would be up against a known terror, one that he had already beaten on the way in.

The cave floor was again flat under his feet, sloping down ahead. Water dripped from tens of thousands of cones made of smooth, cream-colored stone. Some hung from the ceiling like icicles, smaller than his little finger. Others stood as strong, sturdy columns that a dozen men couldn't have put their arms around. He hadn't seen any of this when he was here before, but he did run into a couple of those columns as he stumbled around in the pitch dark. The air was thick with moisture, and a thin layer of slime on the floor made walking treacherous.

As he squeezed through a narrow gap between two rock walls, the rushing air intensified, thickly laced with the smell of wood smoke and roasted meat. He was close now.

Mel trimmed the lantern wick down to a low flame and moved forward cautiously. He was reasonably sure he was at the back of the main entry chamber now, and he scoured his memory for details of the place.

To his best recollection, the chamber was more or less circular, about a hundred feet across. The gaping entrance on the far side was lower than the back side where he was. Chaotic tumbles of stone were all about, but there were dirt pathways among them. On the lower side where the men were camped, the cave floor was flat and clear of rubble.

He moved forward, risking detection by leaving the lantern dimly lit. The embers of two dying fires spaced twenty feet apart glowed and crackled below. The usual snorts, coughs, mumbles and snores of sleeping men were reassuring to him. There was no sign of a guard, or maybe the guard was hidden or asleep. Maybe this useless lot didn't even bother to post one, he realized. They probably felt safe enough in this remote hiding place, knowing that the opposing armies had moved on.

But the big question now was how he would find Rochelle and her sister. As he continued to move carefully forward, it occurred to him that they might not even be here. Or worse, they might be murdered and disposed of already. That thought lit a flame of anger that pulsed through his veins like melted lead. If he found out that that was the case, not a man here was likely to survive the night. It came to him then that this vengeful fire inside of him might be what Ezekiel Adderly expected of his "blood avenger."

He reached the center of the chamber easily enough. Some of the sleeping men were as close as thirty feet away, snoring and shifting restlessly on their stone beds. As he suspected, no man remained awake to watch out over the others.

Then he heard a faint noise close at hand on the right, different than the mix of sounds made by the sleeping men. It was a soft whimpering sound, one like a child might make. He only had to walk a few feet in that direction before a horrible, disgusting scene began to define itself in the dim lamplight.

In a flat open area amid a jumble of boulders, the body of a woman lay motionless on a woolen army blanket spread on the dirt. Her clothes had been torn away, and much of her body lay exposed to the damp night air. She was bruised and filthy, and the blood from a wound on the side of her head had crusted in her tangled brown hair. Her eyes were closed and she lay still as death, though her bare breasts still rose and fell with awful slowness.

Although he barely recognized her, Mel knew it was Rochelle.

A man lay on the blanket beside her, his trousers still down as if, after he had finished his violation of the young woman, he simply rolled off of her and fell asleep. Mel knelt beside the man, staring down at him, burning with silent rage. His hair was long and tangled, and the wiry thatch of his beard covered the bottom half of his face like a rodent sanctuary. A poorly healed scar stretched down one side of his face, as thick and dark as a night crawler. An odor of filth and decay flowed from his open mouth with every noisy breath.

Tangling his fingers in the man's hair, Mel raised his head up about a foot and slammed it down hard on the stone floor of the cave. The man never made a sound, but his breathing stopped immediately. Mel slammed the head down again and again, using all the power in his arms, just for the savage satisfaction of it. Then he shoved the body away, not content to leave it lying on the blanket beside Rochelle.

He tenderly pulled the torn pieces of Rochelle's dress

together to cover her nakedness, then leaned down so his lips were close to her ear. "Rochelle, wake up," he whispered. "It's Mel Carroll."

She didn't move or make a sound. Mel stroked her cheek with his fingers, ready to cover her mouth if she cried out. Her skin was cool to the touch, but not dead cold.

"It's Mel Carroll, Rochelle. I come to take you out of here. You and your sister. Where is she?" There was no response, no movement.

He heard the whimpering again, close now, coming from a shadowy niche in the stone a few feet away. "Oh, please let her be!" a tiny, scared voice begged from that direction. Mel raised the lantern for a better look, and saw what seemed to be a bundle of blankets stuffed back between the rocks. But there was a small white face in the middle of it, with eyes that glowed like a cornered animal's in the lamplight.

"Becky?" Mel asked.

"She can't take no more!" The tiny voice pleaded. "Do it to me if you gotta. But leave her be!"

Mel moved closer to her and she withdrew instinctively deeper into her tight little den.

"Oh, please, mister," the girl whined. "She's had all she can take of this business. I'm a little better off than her, so if you got to . . ."

She was thirteen, Mel thought, or maybe fourteen by now. He tried to close his mind to the thought of all she must have been through since they brought her here.

"Be very quiet and listen to me, Becky. I'm Mel Carroll, your neighbor, and I'm here to take you and Rochelle out of this cave."

"Naw, you ain't real. You're a ghost, or a haint. Or a dream I'm having. Your face is all yellow and red, and kind of shimmery like. You ain't a real flesh-and-bone person."

"Touch my face, Becky," Mel told her. "I'm real enough."

A trembling hand slid out of the folds of filthy blanket, and small fingers brushed his whiskered cheek with the softness of feathers.

"Thank you, Jesus," Becky whispered. "It is you, isn't it, Mel Carroll? But how could you find us?"

"Your mama told me where they took you, and I know these caves."

"Mama? Daddy? Are they still alive?"

"Both alive, and both waiting back at your place." He didn't say any more. They'd see the sad truth of it soon enough when they got back home. But right now this girl needed hope, and the strength it would give her.

"Can you walk?" Mel asked.

"I ain't been out of this hole for a long time," she said. "But I can walk. I will walk."

"All right, you take the lantern and go where I tell you. I'll bring your sister." Mel folded the blanket over Rochelle and picked her up in his arms. She felt like dead weight to him, although he could tell she was still breathing. It felt wonderful just knowing that he had actually found her, and that they were on their way to safety. He made a silent vow that nothing else bad would happen to her, or her sister, as long as he stayed alive to stop it.

But what now? The best exit was right out the front cave entrance. It had been hard enough making it in the back way by himself, and he could hardly imagine what it would be like with an unconscious woman and a scared young girl. But if he tried the front way and woke even one of these men, it would be impossible to fight and run and carry Rochelle all at the same time. It would be over for all of them. With a feeling of dread, he realized what his choice must be.

Becky led the way, moving slowly on stiff, tired legs, and Mel whispered directions to guide her toward the split in the rock at the back of the cave that he came out of minutes before. Once they squeezed through that crack and were clear on the other side, they would be safe. To the band of deserters in the cave, it would seem as if their prisoners had simply vanished.

Weaving through the tangled boulders, Mel wasn't sure where the man came from, but it was clear that they startled him as much as he them.

"Here now, girlie!" a male voice growled out loud. "Where you makin' off to with that lamp?" He grabbed Becky's arm and she seem to go limp in his grasp. For an instant Mel was afraid she would drop the lantern, dashing their hope of escape, but she held onto it.

It was a challenge for Mel to pull his revolver out of its holster without dropping Rochelle, but he managed. His first shot went wild. So did the second and third. He knew he was pulling his shots to the side and high for fear of shooting Becky.

By then the man had fumbled a handgun somewhere out of his own clothing, but as he raised it and fired, a small fist landed hard in his crotch. Doubling over in roaring, cursing pain, he didn't have a chance to shoot again. Mel stepped forward, more deliberate this time, and delivered the kill shot close up.

The rumbling echo of the gunfire got everyone in the cave stirred up in a hurry. Dying fires were kicked back to life, and down toward the cave entrance, Mel could see men rising from their blankets, fumbling for their weapons and staring up toward them.

"What's that shooting?" someone called out. "Who's up there?"

"Head for that crack in the rock, right straight ahead," Mel urgently ordered Becky. "We'll be all right. We'll make it."

He knew he wouldn't be able to carry Rochelle crosswise in his arms through so narrow a passageway. He lowered her to the ground, then he lifted her back up with her arms over his shoulders and her body hanging limp across his back.

Down below men were lighting up lanterns and raising flaming faggots out of the fire. They must have seen the lantern, Mel thought, and it wouldn't take them long to come after him and the girls.

Ahead the light faded as Becky stepped into the cleft in the rock wall. "Don't get too far ahead," Mel warned. "I need to see where I'm going, and I don't want to bang your sister on the rocks."

By the time they made it to the other side and emerged into the next open chamber, Mel could tell that the men were close behind, close enough to make out what they were saying, and to hear the anger and frustration in their voices.

"But we don't know where that crack goes, if it goes anywhere . . ."

"Must go someplace. They went in it . . ."

"Then go in and find out, why dontcha . . ."

"I ain't that curious, an' them two gals was about used up anyway . . ."

"Hell, I'll find out . . ."

Mel stashed Rochelle and Becky off to the side, then knelt by the split in the stone wall. The men on the other side fired a volley into the passageway, but it was a waste of lead and powder. He waited. It took the volunteer several moments of easing carefully forward before Mel spotted the flicker of his lantern and the shuffle of his footsteps.

When the time came, Mel use the same knife thrust he'd used on the loudmouthed scout back in his barn, in just under the point of the breastbone and shoving up. His daddy had highly recommended it, and claimed it had once saved him from a panther mauling. He even had scars across his shoulders to liven up the story.

The lantern the man was carrying fell, splashing coal oil on the stone floor. For a moment the cave was bathed in bright, eerie light, almost blinding to eyes that had grown accustomed to the near darkness. That was a big loss, Mel thought. They sure could have used that lantern to finish their escape from this awful place.

"This one's dead already," Mel called out as the body slumped clumsily to the ground amid the flames. "So you can send me another one. Maybe I'll drag him out into the dark and turn him over to the bats and haints and cave rats." He heard Becky giggle nearby, a sweet, surprising sound.

CHAPTER THIRTEEN

It was nothing short of pure hell finding the way back out of the cave. Rochelle was dead weight all the way. The crawl between the flat layers of rock had been the worst, but at least he had the blanket to drag her along on. Otherwise the harsh layers of stone would have scraped her skin off to the bone. He had thought Becky might balk at snaking through that terrifying narrow space, but it seemed to jangle her nerves less than it did his own.

Eventually the lantern flickered out, which was one of the things Mel had worried about most. But at least it had happened near the end. Becky plunged into complete panic when that last glow of the wick died away and absolute darkness swallowed them. Mel had to grab her and hold her tight in his arms, which seemed like trying to control a writhing, scratching, biting, screaming bobcat. It took a long time before she began to calm down and find her senses again. He promised her over and over that they were all right and would still make it out, and he sure hoped his promises were true.

Finally, as a new day dawned, Mel began to make out a faint glow of light ahead and above. He woke Becky and let her go ahead as fast as she could scramble up the long jumble of stones that led up to the surface of the earth and salvation. It was slower going with the still-unconscious Rochelle, but eventually he reached the top. Then he went back in the cave and fumbled around in the dark until he had retrieved his pack, tossing aside everything except the guns, powder, and shot to lighten the load.

Once outside, the remainder of the trip back to the Adderly farm continued to be an ordeal. Although the distance wasn't that great after they escaped the cave, less than a three-hour walk at a regular pace, it took far longer with Rochelle and Becky.

He fashioned a travois of sorts with the blanket and a pair of long saplings. It seemed like days since he'd last slept, and he knew his body wouldn't hold up to carrying her all the way back. After a couple of hours of slow, bumpy, downhill progress, pulling Rochelle down a narrow game trail and nearly tumbling her off the travois a dozen times, Mel called a halt under the protective boughs of a weeping willow beside a narrow, brisk creek.

Mel fed Becky watercress, wild onions, turnips, and a few little minnows that he managed to seine out of a creek with his shirt. Becky told him she didn't remember the last time she'd eaten. She gulped it all down without complaint, even the flopping little fish, which she swallowed alive and whole. They tickled inside, she told Mel, but not for long.

Rochelle never came around to try the simple food, and Mel's heart sank every time he looked at her. She was bruised and battered from head to foot. Some of the injuries were from the abuse by the men in the cave, but others, he knew, were from the ordeal he had put her through making their escape. Her face was so bruised and swollen that she was hardly recognizable.

Becky poured tiny sips of water into her sister's mouth from time to time, and some seemed to trickle down her throat. Sitting on the damp moss beside the softly breathing form of the young woman he had faced so many hardships to save, Mel fought hard to reject the heartsick notion that, despite all his efforts, the Lord was about to take her anyway. The loss of his cabin and barn, his crops and stock, literally all he owned except a scarred scorched hilltop, seemed like nothing compared to this. He wondered if he'd grieve inside, like Daddy had, for months or years, or right on to the end of his days.

"When they dragged us into that cave, she fought for me long as she was able," Becky said quietly. She had eased up beside Mel, and gently began to bathe her sister's face with the dampened hem of her skirt. "The one you bashed in there, the one beside her, did this to her. He went upside her head with a gun barrel, and she blinked out like a lamp."

"I wish I'd known that," Mel said bitterly. "I'd have made dying a lot worse for him."

The washing reopened a wound above Rochelle's right ear, the one her sister had referred to, and it began to bleed. Becky tore some cloth free from Rochelle's skirt, rinsed it in the creek, and bandaged the long, ugly cut. She seemed to know what she was doing, and didn't squirm at the blood.

Mel recalled a story Mother used to tell about a cousin back home in Virginia who fell off the porch roof, landed on his head, and never woke up again. He'd been up there gathering apple slices that his mother was drying in the sun, when he got careless and fell off backwards. They managed to force enough fresh milk, grits and broth down his throat to keep him alive for weeks, but he never opened his eyes again, or moved, or spoke, or seemed to recognize anybody. That blow was on the back of his head, and Rochelle's was on the side, so Mel prayed it wasn't the same.

"It wasn't all of them," Becky explained. "When they raided the farm, mostly they was looking for food. Twelve or fifteen of them, I guess, ragged and wild-eyed and hungry-looking like wild dogs. Only the one you bashed and a few others wanted to take Ro and me. The rest, I guess, was too scared to argue.

When we got in that cave, that mean one acted like he owned us. He made some of them give him stuff before he let them take care of their business."

"Don't tell me any more right now, girl," Mel said, holding up his hand. "I'm afraid it might make me crazy."

"Maybe Mama will know how to help her when we get back," Becky said. "Some herb teas and poultices, or something like that. Or maybe all she needs is time to rest and heal."

"Maybe," Mel said. He thought of the batty old woman squatting in the dirt plucking a chicken and mumbling nonsense to herself. It didn't seem like she'd have sense enough to help anybody.

"She doctored us all our lives," Becky added hopefully.

Eventually, staggering and falling from fatigue, Becky had to join her sister on the travois during the long trudge back. Mel began to wonder if his own strength would fail him, and he found himself dropping the poles time and again. He had never felt so tired, so weak, and so helpless in all his life. But they did make it back to the farm late in the afternoon.

There was no one in sight as they approached the collapsed barn, but Mel could hear Henrietta talking inside. He called out, and shortly she came crawling out from under the downed building.

At the sight of her mother, Becky tumbled off the travois and stumbled to her. "Mama we're back, we're alive! Mel Carroll took us from them men, and kilt the worst of them in the do- ing," Becky said, throwing her arms around the old woman so suddenly that they both nearly fell. "Ro was thumped on the head, but I know she'll be okay now that we're back home again."

Mel glanced around the wreckage of the Adderly place and thought this wasn't much of a home to return to, but at least they were together again and safe for now.

"I knew you girls oughtn't to be up there in them caves," Henrietta said. "I told your daddy that bad things would come of it. There's bats and snakes and cave rats big as cats . . ."

Surprised by the scolding, Becky drew back and took a fresh look at her mother. Mel watched as the young girl's face clouded with confusion and concern. "Mama, what's the matter with you?" she said with alarm. "Don't you remember those men took us? We didn't want to go."

"I told your daddy . . . ," the old woman continued doggedly.

"Where is Daddy?" Becky asked. "Did his leg get better? We need to take him up to Cable Springs and find a doctor to look at it."

"No need. He's gone on," Henrietta Adderly said simply.

"Gone on to Cable Springs? By himself?"

"He's gone on to meet Jesus, child," the old woman said. "It was his time."

Becky's face went pale and blank with disbelief, and her eyes welled up until a steady stream of tears flowed down her cheeks. She looked at Mel in disbelief, as if he might somehow bear some of the responsibility for Ezekiel Adderly's death.

"By the time I made it here," he said quietly, "it was already too late to do anything. The whole leg was putrified, and it was spreading fast. It's pure mercy that he died quick as he did." Then he added, almost defensively, "And besides, I had to head up to the caves and bring you girls home."

Becky wrapped her arms around her mother and buried her face against her shoulder, sobbing uncontrollably. Motherly instinct took over, and the old woman stroked her daughter's hair and muttered soft consoling words to her. Mel sat down on the dirt beside Rochelle's travois and waited, feeling like an awkward intruder in the grief of this family. He had seen a lot of suffering and dying in these last several days, and was responsible for a share of it himself, but this put a human face on it that he hadn't had much time to think about until now.

When the sharp unexpected pain of loss began to subside, Becky eased away from her mother and managed to turn her thoughts to the situation at hand. She looked down at her sister and said, "One of those men hit Ro in the head, Mama, and she ain't woke up ever since. It's been two days, and Mel and me don't know what to do for her."

"Them caves up there ain't a fit place for no young girls," the old woman said yet again. That one idea was stuck in her brain, and seemed about the only thing left in there. "Bad things was bound to happen . . ."

Becky looked at her mother, seeming to understand, then turned to look at Mel. He could only imagine how her heart must be breaking now, and an absolutely helpless feeling overwhelmed him. He could fight and shoot and do all the hard things a man had to do sometimes to protect himself and those he cared about, but it seemed like there was nothing he could do now to help this girl deal with her pain.

"She was this way when I came through before. This whole thing must have been too much for her, and something broke in her mind. I couldn't bring myself to tell you how bad things were here while we were still up in the hills. But I guess I should have, so you'd have a little time to get ready."

"No, it's okay, Mel," Becky said, reaching out to touch his arm lightly. "You did right. It would have been one more worry."

"We'll take care of her, and your sister, too. We'll do the best we can."

Becky had Mel carry Rochelle down to the bank of the river where there was water. Then he wandered away to give them their privacy. Becky bathed in the river while the old woman bathed and tended to her unconscious daughter with touching tenderness, talking to her all the while, as if Rochelle understood every word. When they called him back, Henrietta Adderly had come up with a white dress from someplace, and managed to clothe her daughter in it. The tattered, filthy rags she'd had on during the trip down from the cave were cast aside on the riverbank. The white dress was dingy and dirty, but Mel could tell that it had once been a fine and special garment. Mel's throat tightened and his eyes went blurry when the old woman explained that it had been her own wedding dress. She was saving it for Rochelle's wedding day.

"Don't worry, Mama," Becky said consolingly. "She'll still wear it at her wedding someday. And maybe so will I."

Mel had to admire Becky Adderly for how she had collected herself together in the midst of all these terrible circumstances. Home and farm lay in total ruins around her, and everyone she cared about was now dead, damaged, or gone. How could a child of thirteen or fourteen have so much come at her so quickly, and still keep her wits about her? In all their lives, Becky and Mel had never exchanged more than a handful of words, and before he led her out of the cave and back home, he felt as if he scarcely knew her. But now he recognized the true strength in her.

Becky crawled into the ruins of the barn and spent some solitary time with her father's body, although the stench drifting out of there by now was almost more than Mel could stand, even from the outside. Mel roamed out into the woods to forage and hunt, and came back with enough to feed them for the night.

They buried Ezekiel Adderly in the little family cemetery, up a grassy slope from where the house had been. Mel dug a shallow grave with a plank pulled from the barn, vowing to return someday with a shovel and do a more fitting job of it. There were no tools to build a coffin but he lined the hole with more random lumber from the fallen barn. Hauling the body up the hillside and into the hole was the hardest part. The stink of the rotting corpse that old Ezekiel's fleeing soul had left behind was nearly unbearable.

He had the hole filled in by the time Becky and her mother returned with wildflowers for the grave. Mel carried Rochelle up to the family cemetery, and held her in his arms while they said good-bye to Ezekiel. It didn't seem fitting to lay her on the ground through all this, as if she was little more than another corpse, waiting her turn.

None of them knew the right words to say, but Becky and her mother sang some hymns, their voices blending with surprising harmony and beauty. Mel knew every word and note they sang, but didn't spoil their familiar harmony by trying to join in. "Amazing Grace," "Take Me Home to Beulah Land," "Through the Dark to Jesus's Arms," and "Death's Sweet Victory." All familiar funeral standards that seemed to add a touch of dignity and finality to the moment.

At one point Mel looked down at Rochelle, and it seemed like he saw her lips moving slightly, as if she was joining in the chorus for her father. His heart leaped for an instant, but then she fell still again, not making a sound. Her eyelids seemed to flutter and he imagined that she might be trying to look at him. But how could he tell for sure through the bruising on her swollen face?

It all seemed so strange and incomprehensible to Mel. He had traveled so far, put himself in all sorts of danger, fought and nearly died, to see, to save, and hopefully to marry, this young woman. Now he stood holding her in his arms, warm and soft, even wearing a wedding dress for heaven's sake, but somehow she seemed farther away than she had been when he first determined to leave his farm and come in search of her. In his mind he cobbled together a simple clumsy prayer for her, as well as for her mother and sister, but he felt like he did a sorry job of it. It probably wasn't deserving of much of the Lord's attention, given everything else that was happening around these parts right now.

Afterward they turned and walked away, Becky clinging to her mother and sobbing. Mel followed, still carrying Rochelle, a dozen thoughts and feelings racing through his mind.

"That was some fine singing you did over the grave," Mel said at last. "I'm sure Mister Zeke would have been proud of the two of you."

"Our family always sang together," Becky said. "Jaipeth had the purest tenor voice you'd ever want to hear, and Ro could sing either alto or soprano, depending on the song."

It bothered Mel that Becky was speaking as if that was all in the past, and the people she mentioned were already gone.

"Seemed to me Rochelle was trying to join in back there at the grave," Mel offered. "And for a second, it seemed like she was trying to look up at me. Prob'ly just my imagination."

"Maybe trying to get a peek at the daddy," Henrietta offered.

"Ma'am?"

"At the daddy," she repeated.

"You mean her daddy?"

"No, no. At the daddy of that new little soul she's carrying around inside of her."

"Becky, what's she talking about?" Mel said.

"You're not the only one who held their tongue on the way down from the hills," Becky admitted, turning to look at him. "By rights it's Rochelle that should tell you. But there's no arguing that you should know, one way or t'other. So now it's out."

For a moment, Mel was too stunned to speak.

"When she missed her time last month, she was so scared she couldn't keep it to herself. She told me, and I told Mama, and Mama told Daddy. After that it didn't take them long to find out from her the when and where and who."

"My Ezekiel was coming for you, boy," Henrietta Adderly said with pride and resolve. "He put a fresh load in the shotgun, and he figured to leave soon as the mare foaled. But then them soldiers come, and all the rest happened."

"I aimed to marry her, anyway, Miss Henrietta," Mel said quietly, "even if I didn't know about the baby." He looked down at Rochelle and said, "I did. I swear to it." Rochelle did not react in any way, nor did the old woman. Mel decided it was time to let things stand as they were, and continued to follow Becky and her mother to the barn.

The sun slid down into the band of trees to the west, and full darkness approached. Mel knew that he had to arrange someplace for them to spend the night. Crawling back into the sanctuary of the fallen barn was no longer reasonable. The stench of death was too much to deal with, and old Ezekiel's spirit, if it hadn't yet moved on to some better place, might get angry about the intrusion. Or it might still be angry about his defiled daughter.

Fresh dead spirits, so people said, weren't something you wanted to mess around with. They didn't have the sense and emotions of real living people, and they hadn't had the time to get used to how they were now. Some didn't even know they were dead yet, or hadn't accepted it. Others were just mad as hell about the whole thing, and ready to take it out on anybody who was handy.

He wondered what it might be like if Rochelle died and he came across her spirit before it traveled on to the heavenly realms. Would she know him? Would she know that he had loved her and wanted to do right by her? Or would she just be another lonely, scary, disconnected soul, angry, resentful of the living, and desperate to cross over to some better place?

He pushed those thoughts out of his mind, realizing that no good could come of them. Mel wasn't sure what sort of damage a spirit might do to a living person, and he didn't want to find out.

Mel made a lean-to by propping up one plank wall of a demolished chicken coop. In the growing darkness they all crowded under it, bone tired, and the three women shared the filthy blanket that Mel had wrapped Rochelle in when he took her from the cave. Mel lay on the ground outside the shelter with one pistol ready in each hand, folded atop his chest. Within seconds the old woman began to snore, a droning nasal rumble that alternated in pitch as the air entered in, then left, her chest. Beside her Rochelle was the same, laying as they put her, like a corpse that still breathed.

Becky lay on the outside, an arm's length from Mel, sniffling softly, uttering an occasional quiet sob. Mel let her alone, understanding that she needed some time to let out all the stored-up fear and grief that she held inside. After a time, she fell still, and Mel thought she had gone to sleep.

"I'm scared they'll come back," Becky said quietly, unexpectedly, as if sharing a secret with the night. Mel had been nearly out, and it took a moment for him to come back awake. "They might be out of food, or they might think they can take me and Ro back. Or they might come looking for revenge 'cause of what you did to their friends."

"They could come back," Mel agreed. "But they'd know that this time a fight was waiting for them if they did. I don't 'spect they'd have the stomach for that. It's why they're up there hiding now, 'cause they ran away from the fighting."

"Even so, they might still stay around these parts and turn into outlaws. There's enough of them to cause a lot of trouble to the folks still left in these parts. And what better place to hide out in than those hills and caves?"

"They don't have time enough left to be a bother to anyone. I've made up my mind about it."

★　★　★　★　★

The moon was perched high in the western sky when Mel woke next. Becky lay close beside him, her head resting lightly on his shoulder, holding his arm in both of hers, snuggled up tight for warmth and safety, Mel figured. He was surprised that she hadn't roused him because he wasn't used to sleeping with anyone. He only allowed the dog, back when he had one, to sleep on the foot of his cot on the coldest nights when the fire had burned down and his feet were cold.

Somewhere in the distance a bobcat snarled, three abrupt, chilling screams, each slightly higher in pitch than the one before. Mel had learned young that a bobcat was an evil-tempered critter, and not to be taken lightly unless you had the means and will to fight to the death. But the screams were far enough away not to be worrisome. Closer around there was only the usual nighttime racket of crickets and frogs, welcome sounds because they meant that there was no other threat close by.

It annoyed him that he had slept so deeply. Anyone could have slipped up on them, and sleeping with a pistol in each hand wouldn't be much help if he didn't wake up in time to use them. By the time he closed his eyes last night he felt so completely exhausted that he figured a black bear could have come sniffing and growling and grumbling around them, and he might not know it until the critter started licking supper crumbs off his face.

After these few days of danger and discomfort, it was hard to imagine bedding down on a fresh straw tick, between clean blankets, with a feather pillow for his head, feeling safe and not needing to keep one ear cocked for the next threat to happen along. He figured it would feel as good as gold coins in his pocket or a new gun.

But those pleasures were still a ways off for him.

Moonlight bathed the landscape of the devastated farm, so bright that he could clearly make out the mound of the fresh grave fifty yards away up the hillside. He would make good time on his way back to the Meat Holler cave.

Mel shook Becky's shoulder lightly and whispered her name, hoping not to rouse the old woman sleeping nearby.

"Mmmm?" the girl responded, still half asleep.

"Wake up, girl," Mel said softly. He pushed her gently away from him so things would be proper. "It's time for me to head back up there and finish this business."

Becky raised her head from the comfort of Mel's shoulder and drew back slightly so she could look at his face. In the moonlight she looked like a child. Her hair was tangled like a handful of straw, and her eyes were full of alarm.

"Now? Tonight?" she asked.

"There's no use waiting," Mel said. "Your daddy named me his blood avenger. I never heard of it then, but now I have an idea what he meant. Men like those up yonder got no right to keep their lives."

He pulled back away so he could see her face more clearly. "Are you comfortable with handguns, Becky? Do you know how to aim and fire one?"

"Daddy taught us."

"All right, I'm leaving one here with you, loaded and ready to shoot. If they come back, keep the gun out of sight until they're close so you have a better chance of hitting someone. At first light, you and your mama put Rochelle on the travois and hide out in the woods someplace close about. Within hollering distance. I should be back by midday."

"And if . . ." The girl hesitated, her voice breaking. "If you don't never . . . I mean . . ."

"If I don't make it back," Mel told her, trying to sound calm, "then you'll have to make do as best you can. Head toward a neighbor's place, or up the post road toward Cable Springs. Don't try to stay here, at least not until the sheriff and some of the local men can clean that bunch out."

Mel rolled away, stood up, and stretched the stiffness out of his body. He showed Becky how to cock and fire the handgun he had given her, then turned it over to her. He shouldered the heavy pack that held the rest of his arsenal.

"If it comes a shower, make sure the loads in that gun stay dry," he instructed. "There's a piece of canvas up in the barn that'll do fine for that."

"I've lived around guns all my life, mister. I guess I know a couple of things about 'em." Becky mustered a smile, and Mel gave her one back. He looked her up and down, holding the loaded revolver in her hand like it belonged there, and thought maybe she wasn't quite the child he had been thinking she was.

"Now you listen to me, Mel Carroll. If things start to go bad for you up there, get away and come on back here. There ain't no law, God's nor man's, that says you've got to finish this thing today, or any other day, for that matter."

"Yes, ma'am," Mel said, grinning slightly.

"Mama and Ro and me need you, mister," Becky said insistently. "You might or might not get this thing done. From what I saw, those men up there ain't much. But you saved us, and now we sorta belong to you. Whether you like it or not. So you make sure you come on back. A live, ordinary man's a lot more use to us than a dead Bible hero."

"Yes, ma'am," Mel repeated.

CHAPTER FOURTEEN

The lookout posted outside the cave sat with his back against the stone wall and his legs stretched out in front of him. Both of his hands rested on the long battered musket that lay across his lap. His head lolled forward, and his blue cap was pulled low over his eyes.

In the dim predawn light the thick ribbon of blood that flowed from the slash across his neck down into his shirt was hardly noticeable.

He was a handsome young fellow, about Mel's own age. Mel guessed that he had probably done pretty well with the girls back home, wherever home had been. He had the soft look of a town boy, and was probably the apple of his mother's eye. The two mistakes that had brought him to this sorry end were probably the biggest he had made in his young life. The first was to run away from the army and take up with this lot. And the second had been to harm, or at least allow his companions to harm, the young women in these parts.

Mel was hidden in a patch of weeds a few feet from the sentry whose neck he had sliced nearly an hour before. He had been dead asleep when Mel crept silently up to him in the dark, and now he was just dead. Wherever he was right now, heaven, hell, or someplace closer about, he was probably still pondering what happened and how he woke up dead.

Mel had spent much of that hour considering when and how to deal with the deserters. When the first gray of morning light began to reveal a little of the cave's interior, he would begin.

In this early, predawn time, an eerie stillness had taken over the woods around him. The nighttime animals and insects had settled into their hidden resting places in anticipation of the new day, and those that lived their lives in the daylight were not yet active. Even the birds hadn't stirred.

He had no doubt that the revenge he was about to inflict, or at least make a try for, was right and justified. Hadn't Ezekiel Adderly himself appointed Mel his Blood Avenger? He was pretty sure that was something straight out of the Bible, and if there was anybody in these parts who knew about God's will and what his Holy Word sometimes required of a man, it was that stern, unforgiving old parson. Yet Mel couldn't ignore the creeping notion that there was a dark and evil side to this business as well, and that somehow the devil also had his hand in it.

This was a terrible thing he was about to do. Some would probably call it straight-out murder. And that didn't take into account the reckless risk he was taking with his own life. He wondered how the men in those armies manage to do it day after day.

He tried hard to hold onto his cold hatred toward the men in the cave for what they had done. No doubt some were evil through and through, but during normal times the rest were probably normal men like him, not going out of their way to harm anybody if they didn't need to.

This day's work was not something that he would ever talk about to anybody, not unless it would be to the Lord himself. But he had to do it.

He didn't try to sneak into the cave like a marauding skunk, in case any of them might be awake and watching. Instead he walked right in, carrying the sentry's musket as if he belonged there. He had his best handgun in a holster at his side, and carried two more hanging from rawhide strips around his neck.

The knife was in its sheath on his belt.

The watch fires had burned down to coals hours before, but there was enough daylight now to make out the dim lumps of sleeping men. Mel moved to one man who slept off a little from the others, and smashed the thick metal butt plate of the musket hard down on his head. Then he moved to another man several paces away and did the same to him.

The second man made a louder gasp than the first as he died, so Mel laid the musket aside and drew his knife to deal with the third. It would be a truly curious and miraculous thing, Mel thought, maybe even a sign from God, if he was able to do away with every blasted man in the cave one by one as they slept. Easy and safe, and leave the mess for the wild creatures hereabouts to clean up.

But that didn't seem likely.

The next man woke as Mel knelt beside him, the bloody knife poised for its work. Instinctively the man grabbed Mel's arm with both his hands and shoved it away from him. Off balance, Mel fell sideways on the stone floor, and in an instant the man was on top of him. By chance Mel's hand closed on the grip of one of his guns. He pointed it up and pulled the trigger. The target was too close to miss.

The man started to scream before the echoes of the gunshot died away in the cave. His blood splashed thick and hot across Mel's face, eyes, nose and mouth. Bitter bile rose in Mel's throat and he tried not to gag. The man fell away, clawing at his face and shrieking out his terror like a dying man, which indeed he was.

And that ended Mel's silent, murderous journey. All around the cave men were tumbling out of their blankets, grabbing for weapons, and staring about in confusion and fear.

"Assassins! They shot Bob!" Mel called out urgently. Every outfit this size was bound to have at least one Bob in it. "They come in the back way, like before."

To make his point, he stood up and cut loose a couple of shots toward the dark recesses of the cave. That set off a brief, earsplitting, and totally pointless fusillade toward the rear of the cave. As they fired, reloaded, and fired again, some of them still in their ragged drawers, hunkered down low, Mel crept over to the nearest group of survivors, a revolver in each hand.

The first moment of panic was passing, and the men began to shout back and forth, trying to figure out where the attack was coming from and how many attackers they were dealing with.

Mel shot one man in the back of his head, and another in his neck as he turned to see who was behind him. A third man nearby stopped in the act of reloading his musket and stared at Mel, realizing in panic that the assassin was not back in the rocks someplace. He was right here, ready to take his life.

"This is for them two girls you took," Mel growled, not really knowing why he bothered to explain. He raised the revolver and pulled the trigger. The hammer fell, but there was no explosion of powder. Misfire! The man threw the musket aside like it was on fire in his hands and fled toward the cave entrance. In seconds he had disappeared into the brush outside, in his panic not even bothering to shout out a warning to his comrades.

Mel knelt behind a jumble of rocks and stuck the revolver back into his holster. He didn't have time to figure out what had happened, but knew he couldn't trust it now. Instead he grabbed one of his neck guns.

In the heat of things he couldn't remember how many he had killed, but he figured there couldn't be too many of them left. Three, maybe four, six at most. But they weren't panicked anymore, and they probably knew about where he was.

"Who the hell are you?" a voice called out.

"I'm God's Avenger!" Mel said. His voice was hoarse and his

heart pounded in his chest like a hammer on iron. "I come to settle with every last one of you skunks for what you did to them girls."

"It warn't none of us! It was Foley and Gale mostly, and a couple of others."

"Then too bad for you."

"I swear to God, mister. I got a daughter myself, and a wife and two sisters. I wouldn't do none of that to them girls, nor would these fellows here, either."

"You have daughters, and still you let that happen?" Mel asked. "Maybe you need to drop your drawers and see if you got anything left down there. Shame on every damn one of you."

"All we want is to leave this cave and head on home."

"That ain't likely," Mel said coldly.

Mel heard the mumble of hushed conversation but couldn't make out the words. It seemed like they were a few dozen feet away, over against the far cave wall, but it was hard to tell because of how the cave twisted and misdirected sounds. He knew he didn't stand much of a chance if they rushed him, especially if they came at him from more than one direction. But he welcomed the chance to have at them one last time. He thumbed back the hammers on both neck guns and waited.

Then they burst from cover, four of them in a tight clump. It took only an instant to realize that they weren't rushing him, but were fleeing instead for the mouth of the cave.

In the few seconds that it took them to scatter into the brush outside, Mel emptied one gun at them, and fetched up the other one ready to shoot. One of them was an older man with gray hair and a twisted, shuffling gait. Though desperate to escape, he immediately fell behind the others. Mel had the best chance of downing him, but fired past him at the others. One fell face forward, skidding in the loose gravel, and then laying still. Another yelped and staggered, but made it into the anonymity of the brush.

Mel switched his aim back to the old man, who was still at least ten strides from safety. He was about Daddy's age, maybe hauled off to the war with no say in the matter. Or maybe a low-down weasel that liked young girls. Mel let him live.

That left three that got away in the brush, one hurt, and maybe some others still hiding in the cave. He knelt and began reloading from the cartridge case on his belt. The fight seemed over, but he wasn't sure. He worked his way back into the darker recesses of the cave, not seeing or hearing any sign of life as he did. He hadn't given much thought to what came after the fight, not figuring on surviving it, he supposed. But here he was.

"Far as I'm concerned this fight's done with," Mel said out loud. The sound of his voice bumped around inside the cave, and he felt very alone. "If anybody's still in here and you have a soul in you, you might want to spend the next few minutes thanking the Lord for letting you live through this one. And I plan to do the same."

CHAPTER FIFTEEN

Away off southeast, Mel could hear the muted throbbing that he now recognized as cannon fire. Not over towards his place, and not near Palestine, either. Farther away than that, maybe down as far south as Sweet Springs. From the sound of things, those Arkansas boys were being pushed back home where they belonged.

Except for Major Elliott, he had no liking for any of them, nor any sympathy for the lives they had squandered on their damned fool errand north. It would have made more sense to Mel if they had been defending their own towns and farms and kin, but that didn't seem to be how this fight worked. Even Elliott, who clearly had plenty of sense and a good heart, seemed kind of confused by the whole thing.

Mel didn't make much better time today on his way back from Meat Holler to the Adderly farm than he had the day before with Rochelle and Becky in tow. He knew he was about used up physically and mentally. More than once he had to pause and grab ahold of some nearby tree while he fought off a wave of dizziness and sorted out the right direction in his head. For days now he had reached down inside himself over and over to find just a little more strength and resolve to push on. But the bucket had finally hit dry rock bottom. The well was empty.

At one point he came to curled up on the ground, not even aware that he had passed out, or fallen to sleep on his feet, or whatever had happened. Laying there for a few minutes, he remembered the dream that his awakening had interrupted. He was back in the cave watching that sad old man hobbling and stumbling, desperate to save what Mel knew at that moment had been a wasted and worthless life. Mel raised his gun and thumbed the hammer back. It was an easy shot. But then the old man was his own daddy, moaning in pain, blood staining the back of overalls, falling down and struggling back up, running desperately for the peace and darkness of the woods. Mel's aim never wavered.

He had been jolted awake by that terrible, impossible decision whether or not to pull the trigger.

For a moment he felt like he might cry, which of course was a silly and weak thing for a grown man to do. He fought back the tightness in his throat and the blurriness in his eyes, rolled over onto his hands and knees, and rose to his feet. His head still swam, but looking around he knew where he was and what direction to go. It was only a little bit farther.

Leaving the woods on the hill above the Adderly farm, the whole place looked deserted. He figured Becky had done what he told her and was hiding out someplace close by with her mother and sister.

It wasn't till he was closer that he saw the still form in the shade of the cottonwoods that sheltered the Adderly family cemetery. And he had to walk closer still before he made out that the form was dressed in white.

At first Mel thought Becky might have left her unconscious sister there, propped up against a tree, while she went off to forage for food. But then, as he approached, he saw Rochelle's head turn slowly toward him.

"So you're back with us again," Mel said, smiling, kneeling beside her, and taking her hand. "That sure is a fine thing."

For a moment Rochelle just looked at him, and Mel had the uncomfortable feeling that she was trying to sort out who he was. Her face was still badly bruised, but the bruises were fading from black to shades of blue and green, and some of the swelling was gone. She still had the rag wrapped around her head, and the wound had bled through. Her hand lay limp, cold, and unresponsive in his.

"Mel," Rochelle said quietly. "Mel Carroll. Becky told me you had come for us, but I don't remember."

"It's 'cause you were knocked out the whole time I was here," Mel explained. "Things will come back to you."

"She told me about Daddy, too," Rochelle said. "She left me here to say good-bye to him. She and Mama are off across the river picking berries. And I heard a shot a while ago, so maybe she kicked up a rabbit."

Mel released her hand and she hid it in the folds of her dress. He sat down cross-legged in the dirt facing her, not really sure what to say. He watched as Rochelle's eyes closed for several long seconds, then opened again and settled on him.

"I said a prayer for Daddy. Or with him, or something like that. It's hard to believe he's laying dead right there under that dirt."

"I know. I felt the same when we buried Mother. But you get used to it."

"Nothing ain't the same now. Everything's changed. The farm's gone like it wasn't never here. Daddy's dead in his grave, and Ham and Jaipeth are off Lord knows where. Even Mama ain't right in the head."

Her eyes swept the empty expanse in front of her that had, just days before, been their family's well-tended farm. Her gaze settled on the rows and rows of graves in what had been Ezekiel Adderly's south pasture. Mel figured they should have planted their dead in plowed ground where the digging was easier.

"For all I know, my own brother Ham might be down there among them," Rochelle mused.

"Maybe not," Mel said. "Maybe he left with them, and he'll find his way home again after all this is done." His words sounded weak even to him.

"It'll be hard to sleep at night, thinking about all them ghosts floating around lost in the dark. It's frightful, but sad too. All them souls, scared and lonely, prob'ly not even knowing what happened to them. And maybe Ham amongst them."

"They'll move on, by and by. It's the same at my place. Plenty of men died there, and they put them in the ground in long rows all over my fields and pastures. They didn't plant them none too deep, either. I guess I'll be plowing up bones from now to doomsday."

Rochelle was quiet for a time, then she turned her gaze back to Mel and asked, "So what now?"

"I figured to take the three of you back to my place," Mel said. "It's not much better there, but I've still got a piece of a cabin standing till I can build something better. My mule should be someplace close about, and my stock is out in the woods. Either I'll herd them back or hunt them for meat. We'll get by."

Mel heard a distant call and turned his head toward the Little Bold River nearby. In the open grassy meadow on the other side he saw Becky and her mother walking in their direction. Becky lifted up the hare she was carrying and waved it in a sign of triumph. Henrietta Adderly was holding up the corners of her apron, which bulged with one sort of victuals or another.

"Once we get there, we need to find a preacher first thing, Mel," Rochelle said. "It's like Daddy said. We had our fun at the dance, and now it's time to pay the fiddler."

"I came all this way with nothing but that on my mind, Rochelle," Mel said. It felt good to get that said. He smiled at her, feeling the certainty of his words, and that felt good too.

"I've been sitting here wondering why all this happened. Do you have any notion of what this was all for, Mel?"

"Nope, it beats the hell out of me, Rochelle."

She turned her head slowly toward him, and her gaze was steady. The look in her eyes changed from sadness to something else.

"I know you've been living for a long time alone, Melvin Carroll, and you've seen some rough times lately. But now you'll be around Christian women again on a regular basis," she said. "You're going to have to save that kind of language for the barn and the fields. I won't abide it."

"Yes, ma'am," Mel said without hardly thinking. In all his pondering of what married life might be like, he had never considered the possibility of living under one roof with three righteous women. He wondered what he had gotten himself into.

ABOUT THE AUTHOR

Over the past thirty-five years **Greg Hunt** has published over twenty Western, frontier, and historical novels, as well as several books on computer topics. A lifelong writer, he has also worked over the decades as a newspaper reporter, photographer and editor, a technical and freelance writer, a tech project manager, and a marketing analyst. Greg served in Vietnam as an intelligence agent and Vietnamese linguist with the 101st Airborne Division and 23rd Infantry Division.

"Writing fiction has been my true, lifelong occupation," said Greg. "The randomness of life and my own restless spirit have steered me in many directions, but since my early years there was seldom a time, even in a war, when you wouldn't find a pencil in my pocket, a piece of paper close at hand, and a plot coming together in my head. I tried to give it up a couple of times when things got rough, but it always kept its grip on me until I finally realized that I could never *not* be a writer. My first rule of writing is as simple as it gets. *Tell a Good Story.*"

Greg currently lives in the Memphis area with his wife Vernice.